IOTA

T. M. Doran

IOTA

A Novel

IGNATIUS PRESS   SAN FRANCISCO

Cover design and artwork by Milo Persic

© 2014 by Ignatius Press, San Francisco
ISBN 978-1-58617-854-3
Library of Congress Control Number 2013916526
Printed in the United States of America ∞

June 20, 1990

Discordance: heaps of rubble and linen-covered tables; construction equipment growling, belching smoke; people quietly chatting at café tables; the Wall coming down and table umbrellas going up; and ominous clouds on the horizon and sunshine in the *platz*.

Accordance: two men sitting at a table observing the demolition of the Wall, eating cheese, grapes, and walnuts as if the incongruity of the scene were the most natural thing in the world.

Though the two men had been conversing in English, one man, the larger of the two, could be identified as Russian by his accent. The other man's origins were more difficult to identify because his speech suggested a mixture of tongues: now Russian, now French, now Irish-English, now another Slavic language. The Russian, still robust though advanced in years, wore a drab-colored shirt with a fraying collar beneath a gray jacket. His white hair was short, and he was hatless. He had big, wrinkled hands and pale blue eyes. It was not a cold day, but the smaller man wore a wool navy blue coat. His eyes were dark and recessed, but lively. He might have been a handsome man when he was young. He too was hatless, and his hair was gray laced with wheat-colored strands.

The man in the blue coat said, "Is there a washroom inside?"

"Yes, but very small."

"I have made do with less, as you recall."

"It was regrettable." The Russian seemed to mean it.

Several of the patrons watched the man in the blue coat with interest, or amusement, as he made his way into the building. The Russian lit a cigarette, took a few puffs, and put it out. While his companion was away, a second round of drinks was served: vodka for the Russian and Riesling for his companion.

The man returned, and the two touched glasses, saying nothing for several minutes, watching the people stroll by on the sidewalk and the construction workers labor across the way. People of all ages were walking up and down the street, moving with purpose. Many stopped to watch the deconstruction of the Wall. Some cheered.

A cool breeze began to stir the umbrellas; lightning streaked across the western sky. The smaller man fastened the top button of his coat. Involuntarily shuddering, he recalled an encounter with Vyacheslav Molotov, who traveled to Prague in 1945 to meet Edvard Beneš, the titular president of Czechoslovakia. The Soviet minister of foreign affairs had invited him, a journalist in those days, to the Soviet embassy. The journalist had been excited about the prospect of meeting Molotov; but as it turned out, the interview was short, even perfunctory. The answers of the dour, mustachioed Molotov had been murky at best.

"Will the Soviet Union accept a democratic Czechoslovakia?" the reporter had asked.

"Of course," Molotov had said, "the general secretary has said so."

"It is said that the Soviet Union is arming the communists."

"Nonsense."

"Then the Soviet Union will accept a democratic Czechoslovakia according to the Western model?"

"What Western model, my friend? France, Italy, and Germany will be socialist republics like those of the USSR before long; perhaps England too."

"Do you think so?"

"Europe is eager to embrace the Soviet model. The Czech people should hear this. You should tell them."

Wrenched back to the present by the rat-a-tat-tat of a jackhammer, the man in the blue coat said, "Forty-five years is a batting of the cosmic eye—less than that."

"I know nothing about cosmic eyes. I am a simple man." The Russian grinned broadly, lifted his glass, and sipped.

6

A fly perched momentarily on the rim of the wine glass, and the man in the coat almost upset the glass with a swipe at the insect, saying, "I cannot abide insects in my food."

"I understand, my friend", the Russian said.

"There are lessons that are hard to unlearn", the smaller man said with a sigh. He began speaking in Russian, but his companion put up a hand and said, "English—you know the rule."

"All right, if that's what you prefer."

"Let it be so. One of my sons teaches English, and all my grandchildren are fluent in English. I am as comfortable speaking English as an uneducated man can be."

"Education is not everything. . . . The major was an educated man."

The Russian smiled, showing his teeth, those that remained. His weather-beaten face was not without interest. An old scar was visible on his forehead. He had the appearance of a man who had seen and done much.

A woman holding a piece of concrete as big as a melon walked past their table. At that moment, the proprietor approached them and greeted them in German. The Russian shook his head and said, "English!"

"Are you comfortable . . . outside?" asked the café owner.

The Russian nodded his head, and the other man said yes.

"The dust and noise are terrible", the proprietor observed. "Sometimes we must stop serving out here."

"It will be over soon", the man in the blue coat said.

The proprietor gave him a condescending look and said, "Not soon enough. Before long, these *Mauerspechte* will be walking off with my chairs and umbrellas." The man swiped the tabletop with a cloth and moved away.

The late afternoon sky flashed with light, and thunder rumbled in the distance.

"Whatever happened to that lovely guttersnipe?" the smaller man asked.

"What is a guttersnipe?" the Russian asked in return.

"A woman who specializes in deceit."

The Russian pondered this question before he said, "She dressed up nicely, but it did not improve her ... disposition."

The smaller man looked up at the approaching storm clouds and turned up his collar. He hated the cold. He had vowed that he would never be cold again if he could help it. He looked into the wineglass and said, "This is a good Riesling."

"I will take your word for it. I do not care for wine. I might have been executed on account of wine." The Russian turned toward the construction workers and added, "The owner of this café might be unhappy about the Wall, but I would not be here otherwise. Russia is my home, and I will return there; but to be free to go west— that is something I never expected."

"Vaclav Havel and the others are demanding freedom in Czechoslovakia. Havel is a moral force; I expect him to succeed. Many more people will be free to go west before long.... So, tell me more about your family."

"Four boys, and they have made me a grandfather ten times, and the great-grandfather of six. And you?"

"I never married. I ran as far as possible from that place. In Dublin, I taught French and Russian at Trinity College."

A boy and a girl, skipping and holding hands, came down the sidewalk, attracting the attention of the two old men. The blond-headed pair stopped a stone's throw from the men's table to watch the construction crew. The girl pointed to the Wall and asked the boy a question, while he mimicked a bird pecking at the pavement by hopping up and down and bobbing his head.

The smaller man said to his companion, "Whatever became of those pitiful orphans?"

The Russian frowned and shrugged his shoulders. "They were shipped out the same day they arrived; we were merely a way station. I put the last of my chocolate into the boy's pocket before they departed."

The waiter came to the table and asked if they wanted anything else to eat. "No," said the man in the blue coat, "but two more drinks, if you please." Then he said to his companion, "We are celebrating."

The Russian nodded vigorously and emptied his glass. He licked his lips and said, "You have been living in Dublin ever since—"

"Yes."

"I have read that Dublin is a friendly town."

"You could say so. It was out of the way."

"When will you return?"

The blue-coated man leaned forward and said, "I am returning to Ireland in two days. Speaking to you has brought back harsh memories. I am again reminded of those war years. A man can find a kind of peace—a distracted peace—with the false image of himself he has in his imagination. It takes a big event, a catastrophe, to dislodge this image."

There were fewer people in the street, and the remaining patrons who had been sitting outside were moving indoors. The drinks arrived, the remnants of the food were removed, and the sky grew darker. The smaller man moved his hand to the top button of his coat before he remembered that it was already fastened.

More lightning, and the thunder that followed was louder than before, but neither man exhibited any inclination to move.

A stranger approached. He too was old, and he wore a black suit and a thin black tie. The stranger hadn't shaved for several days, and wavy white hair cascaded from beneath his hat. He didn't seem to be in a hurry, but he moved with determination. He retrieved a chair from another table and sat with them. In the shadow of his hat, his slate blue eyes were vacant, without any discernible spark of vitality. He said, "A bad storm is coming."

As if to reinforce the stranger's observation, a loud peal of thunder erupted overhead. Rain began tapping on the umbrella, and all three men instinctively moved their chairs toward the center of the table.

"Would you like something to drink?" the man in the blue coat asked the newcomer.

"Nothing."

"You do not have an umbrella."

"I do not use one."

"You are welcome to sit with us until the storm passes."

9

"Will it pass?" The stranger turned his head and stared at the disintegrating Wall. The workers had gone to find shelter, and the equipment was quiet. Waving his hand before the scene, the man said, "This reminds me of ants moving their debris."

The man in the coat said, "Not ants and not debris. I have come a long way to witness this event."

"I know that you have. Are you having a pleasant reunion?"

When neither of the two answered, he continued, "I have been watching you."

"May I ask why you have been watching us?" asked the man in the blue coat.

"Because you are the reason I am in Berlin."

The Russian gulped the last of his vodka and set the glass down hard on the table. He said, "Who are you? What do you want?"

The stranger put his hand in his pocket and slowly removed a pistol, old but well preserved. He gently placed it on his lap and said, "Don't you recognize me?" He gave them barely a second to answer before saying, "No matter. I have come to kill you. I have come to kill both of you."

November 1, 1945

Jan had heard three doors close in the past thirty-six hours, and each closing had magnified his sense of desolation. A fourth door, the one to his flat in Prague, had been left open when they had hustled him out in the middle of the night with the muzzle of a pistol pressed against his temple and his arm pinned behind him. The door of the black sedan, after he had been pushed into the backseat, had made a barely audible click as it closed, suggesting well-oiled hinges and clasps. The door to the transport truck, after he had been herded into the rear with a dozen other dazed and terrified men, had rattled raucously as it had been lowered. Lastly, the door to his cage had banged shut after he had been shoved inside. He would never hear a door close behind him again without experiencing a wrenching sensation in his gut.

The plainclothesmen who had forced their way into his apartment had commanded him in Czech, but he had understood them perfectly when they had spoken Russian to each other because he had majored in languages at university and was fluent in Russian, French, English, Italian, and German. The men were making a terrible mistake, Jan had told them; he was not German or a Nazi. Several times, he had asked them why they were apprehending him, where they were taking him, but they had ignored his entreaties.

When armed Russian soldiers had directed him to exit the truck, Jan had noted the expressions of the other captives in the vehicle: envy that he was he being released from the suffocating darkness, pity that he might be going to his execution, fear that they too might be killed.

The relief Jan had experienced in the fresh air and sunlight had soon been replaced by dread as he had been pushed past piles of rubble into an industrial building that appeared to have miraculously survived Allied bombing. Using metal fencing topped with barbed wire, the Russians had crudely divided the interior into cages, not for animals, but for men.

"What did you do to deserve to come here?" the man on the opposite side of Jan's cage asked in English. He was older than Jan, perhaps forty, of average height, stocky, with gray-blue eyes and dark wavy hair. This man was wearing a blue work shirt, brown trousers, and black boots. From the looks of his facial hair and clothing, he did not appear to have been imprisoned for long.

Polish, Jan concluded from the man's accent. "Nothing", he replied, also in English.

"I am waiting to hear something original", the man remarked. Though caged, there was no hint of subservience in this man's lively eyes.

"It is the truth in my case", Jan said with passion.

"What is truth?" the man asked, rhetorically, it seemed to Jan. "In such a place as this, truth is survival, nothing more nor less."

Deciding that acting as normally as possible was the best course of action, Jan said, "I am Jan Skala", and extended a hand.

"Jerzy Drewniak", said the man, leaving Jan's hand unclasped. Then Drewniak smiled and pumped Jan's hand heartily.

"Why are you speaking English?" Jan asked.

"Our *host* has ordered it. No other language is allowed, except for the guards."

"And if you cannot speak English?"

"Then you may not speak. Rather, you dare not speak."

"Why such a rule?"

"Our jailers are not in the habit of explaining themselves."

"Wouldn't they prefer many languages? Less opportunity for plots."

"I do not think our jailers are afraid of plots," Drewniak answered, "but prisoners who speak English might find that understanding the conversations of other prisoners is useful."

"Pit one against the other?"

12

"Of course", Drewniak said. "This is my own idea, understand. All you need to know is that the rule is enforced. The guard Evgeny caught Lutz speaking German and beat him with his stick. Lutz did not say a word in any language for several days. That lesson was not lost on the rest of us."

"Who cannot speak English?"

"Who can say for sure? That old man", Drewniak pointed at a bearded man two cages away wearing a homespun sweater and green trousers, "and his cagemate do not speak. All the others speak English. Surprising, wouldn't you say?"

"Yes, and I will try to remember the rule", said Jan.

"Forgetfulness earns the same punishment as disobedience. I would not forget if I were you."

Jan observed that there were few prisoners in this large building and that, besides Drewniak, only one took an overt interest in his arrival, a man in a cage diagonal to Jan's, a spare man, probably in his fifties, with a steep forehead, large round eyes, and graying brown hair. This prisoner had a mostly bald cagemate wearing a red and white checked shirt.

The stench was overpowering, and Jan felt like retching. Besides the smell of unwashed bodies and excrement was a cloying, sickly sweet aroma. He asked, "What is this place?"

Drewniak didn't answer right away. The Pole looked up at the rafters and the catwalks that passed over some of the cages, including their own; then he put his hands behind his back and said, "What is it ... or what was it?" Not waiting for Jan to answer, he replied, "It was an abattoir; swine, I think. When I was a boy, my uncle had an abattoir near Krakow. I grew accustomed to this vile odor in my uncle's shop. One can get accustomed to almost anything."

Jan told himself that he could never, ever get used to a place like this.

The Pole withdrew his hands from behind his back and said, "Unless I am mistaken, we are on the hide-processing floor. That means the cutting floor is behind our neighbors' cages. The areas near the back wall were probably for the tallow ... and the boilers."

Pointing to pipes on the surface of the concrete floor and passing through each cage, he said, "Warm water from the one operating boiler runs through these pipes, the only source of heat these days. We flock to these pipes at night as moths to a light bulb."

"Your English is very good", Jan said.

"I learned to speak in primary school and improved my skills at the University of Krakow. I never finished my studies, but the English stuck."

Jan did not reveal that he was a polyglot. He had always had a natural aptitude for languages, even before attending university. His father, a newspaper publisher, had hired Jan in part for his language skills. Jan proved himself a capable journalist, and he resented when people assumed that his father alone was responsible for his success.

"Is there anything to read here?" Jan asked Drewniak.

"You will not find any reading material in this place, or eyeglasses. It is one of the barbs these Russians inflict on us."

No books or newspapers? Jan could not remember a day when he hadn't spent at least an hour reading, even during the darkest hours of the war. He could not imagine life without something to read.

Apart from the rusty pipes on the floor, the only thing in the cage was a chamber pot. The sight of it made Jan realize that he needed to relieve himself, but the thought of doing it in the open with all of these men watching appalled him.

As if reading his mind, Drewniak said, "The first few times are difficult. After that, you hardly notice, and no one else gives a damn. Just hope your bowels keep working."

When he had finished with his latrine, Jan sat in the corner of the cage with his back to the fence. Surely his captors would soon realize the mistake they had made, he thought, or his father would learn of his arrest and secure his release. Meanwhile he must figure out how to survive a night, a late autumn night, in this cold place without a blanket. Drewniak had said that the pipes were warm, but he couldn't feel any warmth from where he sat. He had an urge—a strong, panicky urge—to shake the wire and shout for the guards, to demand that they bring him to someone in authority. Suddenly music started: loud, not earsplitting but not soothing either, martial music.

If this had once been a meatpacking plant, almost all of the equipment had been removed. What remained were some tanks and debris in the corners. Jan could see only one man door, the one through which he had been conveyed. At the opposite end of the building was a big roll door for trucks.

A guard and a hunched old man entered the building. The guard carried a rifle, and the old man pushed a wheeled cart that supported an open-top fifty-five-gallon drum.

Drewniak whispered to Jan, "That is Herr Shithauler."

The two men went from cage to cage. The guard covered the prisoners with the rifle while the old man emptied the chamber pots into the drum. There was no cleaning of the pots or the stained floors, just emptying and moving to the next cage.

"Where is this place?" Jan asked, fighting back revulsion and terror.

"Somewhere near Berlin, I think."

Drewniak might be correct, Jan admitted to himself, judging by the time he had spent in the truck.

Another guard, a giant of a man in his thirties with hair the color of ripe corn and an angry scar on his forehead—Piotr by name, according to Drewniak—brought each of the prisoners a metal bowl filled with a lukewarm soupy substance. Jan sniffed it, but did not consume it. "Is this all we get?" he asked Drewniak.

"Sometimes we get moldy bread with our ... soup. They give us just enough food to keep us breathing. It is all part of the program: break us, destroy our wills, empty us of all our secrets."

"I have no secrets", Jan fumed. "I am not a Nazi and never have been. I welcomed the Russians."

Before the liberation of Prague by the Russians, the Nazis had controlled Jan's newspaper. The Gestapo officer who had "retired" Jan's father had vanished before the Russians entered the city. Jan could not help being worried about what his past association with the German occupiers might suggest to the Soviets.

"Perhaps our captors already know that you are not a Nazi", Drewniak said.

The thought that the Soviets knew he was not a Nazi and had still abducted him frightened Jan more than anything else he had considered. His hope had hinged on the Soviets having mistaken him for an enemy. Why else would they have taken him? Did they believe that he deserved imprisonment, or even death, for doing only what he had been compelled to do? Had he not, after a fashion, been cooperating with the Russians, just as he had cooperated with the Nazis before them? This Russian intrusion was supposed to be different. They were the liberators of the Slavs. Many insisted it was only a matter of time before the Slavs would have their country back now that it was no longer part of the Reich.

Jan, however, had already seen and heard too much to believe that the Soviets cared about the aspirations of his countrymen. Just months earlier, shortly after Laurence Steinhardt had taken up residence at the Schönborn Palace as the American ambassador, Jan had visited the man to interview him, and he had found the American distracted and terse. Jan had left the meeting worried that the Americans would fail to check the Soviets.

Jan knew the communists, the CPC, to be well-organized and fervent Marxists, while the democrats were disorganized. Jan's father feared a communist coup, and while Jan had been disinclined to this view, he had been less confident of a robust Czech democracy after his meeting with Steinhardt than he had been earlier. Less than a month before he was abducted, Jan had interviewed Masaryk. Though the Czech foreign minister had done his best to affirm the sound relationship between his country and the Soviets, there had been an unspoken undercurrent of anxiety in his statements.

Despite these apprehensions, Jan was trying to convince himself that the Soviets would not consider him an obstacle or a threat. Thus Drewniak's implication that the Soviets knew something incriminating unnerved him.

"If they know I am not a Nazi, why am I here?" Jan demanded. "I am a journalist and a Czech patriot."

"The Soviets have no use for patriots", Drewniak glibly responded.

"But we helped them defeat the Nazis." This was the line Jan knew he must take at all costs.

Drewniak shrugged dismissively.

Jan supposed it was early evening but had no way of knowing. All of the windows had been boarded up, and each of the cages was fitted with bright lamps. "What time do they shut off the lights?" Jan asked Drewniak.

"We have bright light and loud music all day and all night. It is part of the therapy."

"Torture, you mean to say", Jan erupted.

Drewniak's mischievous eyes twinkled. "Depends on one's view."

"How can you have such an attitude?"

Drewniak ignored Jan's question, saying, "God, I could use a cigarette. I don't suppose you have any."

Jan shook his head and began examining the other cages. To his right, a bald, flabby man in his sixties, wearing a soiled nightshirt and navy trousers, was waddling around his cage. The other prisoner in that cage was a thin, curly-haired man with stiff gray eyebrows. Wearing a red V-neck sweater vest over a gray shirt, the man was hunched in the back of his cage.

As Jan turned to the forward cage, he heard Drewniak say, "God knows how a Chinaman found his way here. His bedfellow, Nagy, is Magyar nobility, or so he claims. These days, every wretched lizard wants us to believe he is descended from *Tyrannosaurus rex.*"

The Chinese man seated at the far side of the cage was young and lithe. Curiously, he was wearing the drab olive shirt and pants of a Russian soldier. Rather short and pudgy, the man Drewniak had called Nagy sported a thick black moustache and a longish billy goat beard. Although the man had the wearied appearance of someone who looked older than he actually was, Jan guessed he was in his forties.

Drewniak said to Jan in a confidential voice, "Nagy had a bad case of delirium tremens soon after he arrived. The absence of drink, I suppose. I myself admit to having felt shaky for the first few days."

"I saw you leering at our Katrina", Nagy said loudly to the man with the steep forehead and round eyes, the man who had taken an interest in Jan at his arrival. "I wonder if you would know what to do with her."

Was there a woman in this place? Jan scanned the building and saw a curled-up form several cages distant that could have been a small man or a woman.

"A tiresome wretch, that Nagy", Drewniak said, seemingly unconcerned that the man could hear him. "He needs to be more careful, or he will end up on the wrong end of a gun. I have loosened men's teeth for less than what this man has said.... These are brutal times, Skala. If there is a way out of here, it is playing whatever game the Soviets want us to play."

Facing Jan, he added, "That is my angle, and it will be yours if you are smart."

Two men occupied the cage to Jan's left. One, a small, blue-eyed man in his fifties, wearing a grimy white shirt and black slacks, sat on the floor with his arms around his knees. The other man was a hardier specimen, big boned and tall. He stood in the center of the cage and was scratching his head vigorously.

In fact, many of the men were scratching their heads or their armpits, Jan noticed. Lice, he supposed, as he reached for the back of his neck.

The blue-eyed, white-shirted man on the floor, who had been listening to Drewniak, said in German-accented English, "This is quite a collection of specimens. Considering the shortage of building materials, the Russians have gone to some trouble with this place. I ask myself why."

"Vermin", his big cagemate said, causing Jan to wonder if he were referring to the prisoners or something else.

Later—whether night or day, he had no way of knowing—Jan awoke on the hard floor. He was cold and stiff in spite of pressing as much of his frame as possible against the warm water pipe; his head was throbbing. How he had managed to sleep was a mystery.

The bright light caused him to shut his eyes again but not before he observed a rat scuttling through an adjacent cage.

In spite of the amplified music, he was sure that someone was singing: a woman. Her plaintive song contrasted with the jarring noise emitted by the loudspeakers. The man called Nagy had mentioned a woman. Who was she?

The night he was arrested, Jan remembered, he had been listening to a woman singing Czech folk songs on the radio and had fallen asleep in his favorite chair. He was rudely awakened by a towel over his mouth and the business end of a pistol against his temple. Four men looking like bankers or schoolteachers in their gray suits and ties were admonishing him to be silent, to get dressed quickly, and to bring nothing.

He remembered one man more vividly than the others, not because the man was more voluble than the rest or did anything particularly aggressive but because he had reminded Jan of his uncle, the cardinal: those small, delicate spectacles and the benign expression, as if he were doing something distasteful, but a deed that had to be done.

The singing stopped, and someone was weeping, sobbing restrainedly rather than wailing, as if the person were ashamed to cry but could not help himself. Jan felt something scurry over one of his legs and cried out.

Would he ever sleep again as he had in his own home? Of course he would, after the Russians realized their mistake, but he could not help wondering if he would ever see Frantiska again. Occasionally, he had questioned if he really loved her. She was pretty, and he enjoyed her company, but did he love her? How had she taken his disappearance? How had his father and friends taken it for that matter? Surely, he insisted to himself, they would realize that his disappearance was not his own doing. They must be seeking him.

November 2, 1945

Jan stepped into a room that looked as if it had once served as the abattoir's general manager's office. For the first time since he had been hustled into the truck, he felt warm all over. Though marred in places, the wood floor retained some of its varnish, and the paneled walls were in good condition. The desk was large and of good craftsmanship, though not ostentatious. It was flanked on either side by brass standing lamps, both illuminated. Two windows, one on the entrance door wall and the other to Jan's right, looked out on the yard. The room contained no decorations or art, suggesting that its former occupant had been austere or had removed these things when the enterprise ceased operations.

The leprous landscape Jan had seen on his way to this building consisted of a gravel yard defaced by refuse and rusting equipment, an area that might once have served as animal pens, a trio of smaller outbuildings, and railroad tracks. Small farmhouses were scattered in the open fields at some distance from the compound. A stench, though of a different kind from that of the abattoir, had emanated from a mist-enshrouded pond—probably a sewage pond—near the former pens.

The man seated behind the desk, examining Jan through thick-lensed glasses, reminded the prisoner of a pale frog. His shaved head was a gleaming dome, but the skin on his face was gray, lusterless, and smooth, like that of a man for whom growing facial hair is problematical, if not impossible. His eyes, wide set and magnified behind the lenses, were expressionless. Sitting erect, his hands hidden behind the desk, the man was wearing a green military shirt, tieless and open at the neck, with major's shoulderboards.

The major raised a hand, causing Jan to halt, and when the man spoke he might have been a ventriloquist, so little did his lips move. "You may leave us", the major said to the guard in English, revealing a tinny voice at odds with his bulky torso.

Jan did not look behind him, but the guard must have been slow in obeying the order, because the major's eyes flashed, and, in a voice that rose several octaves, he said, "Go now."

Jan heard the door close. He expected the man to say something to him, but the major sat silently, observing Jan as a cat might observe a caged bird. There was a chair in front of the desk, but the major did not invite Jan to sit.

"Of course, it is a mistake that you are here", said the major.

Jan had thought about what he would say when he was afforded the opportunity to speak to someone in authority and had decided, after experiencing the prisoners' lot, to hold nothing back. "Yes, a mistake", he said. "Mr. Molotov received me. He did not consider me a criminal ... or an enemy."

"Ah", the major said, smiling and nodding.

"Mr. Molotov might vouch for me if you will allow me to contact him." Jan was not certain the minister would even remember him, but he was grasping at anything that might convince the major the Soviets had made a mistake in arresting him.

"I am certain the minister of foreign affairs is occupied with important matters. If we have made an error in detaining you, it will soon be corrected."

Jan's impression was that these words had been said as a formality, with no conviction, so he replied in Russian, "As you say, Major."

The major's thin lips compressed to a barely perceptible line. "We will speak English. You will speak English at all times. This is not a request. The rule fosters order. Do you know what they told me about you?"

"I am a patriot", Jan insisted. "Patriotism can lead to misunderstandings."

"Your English is good. So is mine. As to misunderstandings, how well I know it. What would you do to be released and sent home?"

"I am ready to tell you everything to convince you that this is a mistake."

"Everything?" the major said. "You would be a rare man if you told me everything, nor would I presume to ask it of you. I am a simple officer on the fringe of big events. What I need to know is modest."

Jan's mind was spinning. A *simple* officer speaking fluent and subtle English?

"Here", the major said, opening a drawer and laying a cigarette case, silver with red filigree, on the desk. "Do you smoke?"

Jan shook his head.

"Please be seated." A command presented as a request.

The major removed a cigarette from the case, lit it with a lighter that possessed a similar pattern, took a long draw, and emitted a dense cloud of smoke, knocking the ashes on the floor. "I want to demonstrate my goodwill." He reached behind the desk for an opened bottle of wine, three-quarters full. He produced two glass tumblers and filled them with several inches of the purple-red liquid. "I was told this Bordeaux came from Goering's cellar. Will you join me?" The major slid one of the tumblers toward Jan.

Jan reflected that if they wanted to kill him, there were easier ways than serving him poisoned wine. He took a sip and found the wine to be good.

The bald man swirled the wine in his tumbler and inserted his small round nose into the glass as he might have done in a fine restaurant. "Tell me about yourself", the major said.

Jan was still wearing the shirt and slacks he had been rushed into putting on when he was arrested. He looked down at his grimy cuffs and muddy shoes.

"I am a journalist", Jan said, lifting his head. He suspected the major already knew this. "I resisted the Nazis."

"Come now. We both know you ... ah ... accommodated the Germans."

"I did only what was necessary to stay alive."

"You accommodated that dog, Frank", the major observed nonchalantly.

Chief of police for the Protectorate, Karl Hermann Frank; how much did this man know?

The major asked Jan, "Where is your father?"

The tumbler was at Jan's lips. He was sure the major noticed his surprise.

"Would you care for more wine?" Without waiting for Jan to answer, the major added a generous measure to his tumbler. Jan was so shaken by the question about his father that he wasn't sure he could get the glass to his lips without spilling the wine.

"He was home when I was—"

"Summoned."

Jan nodded and swallowed.

"He did not tell you that he was planning to leave Prague?"

Was the major telling the truth, or was this a tactic to evoke something from him? "He never mentioned leaving the city", Jan said.

"Doesn't that seem strange, considering you are his only child?"

"Yes," Jan admitted, "if he has truly left Prague."

"How do you explain it?" the major inquired.

"I cannot explain it."

"Try", the major said insistently. "The alternative to honesty is unspeakably depressing."

Jan was balancing an eagerness to accommodate his captor with caution. His father had always kept his own counsel. If his father had left Prague, it must have been for a good reason. Jan took another sip of wine, set the tumbler on the table, and said, "Perhaps he learned that I was ... summoned and felt compelled to leave."

"That is possible. Do you think it is the truth?"

"I cannot think of any other reason for my father to leave Prague", Jan said resolutely. He did not add that he had never really understood that complex man.

"Very well", the major said, taking a sip of wine. "You said you would tell me everything. I am taking you at your word ... for now. What do you think of your fellows?"

He must be referring to the other prisoners. Jan said, "I barely know them. I have scarcely said a word to any of them."

"Not even to Drewniak? I advise you to be careful with that one."

"Is he dangerous?"

"He might be ... to you. Have you spoken to Charlie Chan?"

"Who?"

The man beamed a smile at Jan. "I studied electrical engineering at Purdue University in the middle United States. At the dormitory, we were sometimes entertained with motion pictures. Charlie Chan is a fictional Chinese detective who solves mysteries and dispenses witty ... um ... *epigrams* might be the word."

No wonder the major's English was so good.

"*Your* Charlie Chan is no detective or sage, needless to say," the major added, "but it pleases me to recall those films."

"How did you find America?" Jan asked, daring to hope that his captor had absorbed some liberality from his time at an American university.

"The experience was useful. Have you met Brandt?"

When Jan displayed ignorance, the major said, "Brandt shares a cell with another German named Schreiber. Brandt was a Gestapo colonel, a very active villain."

Though he had not yet heard the name, Jan thought of the tall German in the next cage. He said, "The Nazis invaded and brutalized my country: Heydrich and his thugs."

The major chuckled and relit his cigarette. "Heydrich and his thugs ... would that description include your friend Frank?"

Jan wanted more wine but checked himself. Perhaps the major noticed, because he made a move to refill Jan's tumbler, demurred, then recorked the almost empty bottle.

"Do not be tempted to think that because I studied in America, I experienced a privileged youth. Hardly that. I was fifteen years old when revolution consumed Russia. Moscow was in chaos, utter chaos. We were compelled to move every few months."

"You remember that I spent the war in Prague", Jan said.

The major smiled indulgently and continued. "Streets in ruins. Black market princes. Fences, benches, even bannisters from fine homes taken apart for fuel. Motorcars replaced by sleds in those bitter winters. Starvation, deprivation, typhus. Fighting between reactionary forces: villains like Brandt versus heroes of the revolution. I witnessed all of it.

"If your papers weren't in order, or if you were in the wrong place at the wrong time, or if you annoyed the wrong person, you could be taken by a work gang and transported to one combat zone or another."

Was the major trying to show that the two of them had something in common, or was he merely attempting to give his own actions a veneer of legitimacy?

"And the wolves at night ... ravenous. They came into the towns and villages. In those times, it did not pay to be out of doors at night.

"Now where were we?" the major said. "Your father has disappeared. I am sure we will find him at one border or another."

"He did not flee during the war."

"There is that. What do you know about Trotsky?"

Jan sensed that this question was more than an aside, in spite of the offhand manner in which it was posed. "Trotsky collaborated with Lenin."

"True, so far as it goes. Do you associate with any of Trotsky's ... ah ... disciples?"

"Not to my knowledge."

"Consider carefully."

Jan mentally went through a list of his close friends. There were fervent socialists among them, but he couldn't recall anyone being a follower of that Russian revolutionary. "I recall reading that Trotsky was murdered in Mexico", Jan said to the major.

"Executed, not murdered. Please answer my question."

Jan possessed what many called a photographic memory: not the perfect recollection many imagined, but an exceptional talent for recalling past events and what he had read and heard. "To the best of my knowledge, none of my friends are followers of Trotsky."

"If you happen to remember something, I would be glad to hear it", the major said. "Are you familiar with the term *gulag*?"

Jan said, "No, I am sure I have never heard that word."

"Never heard it", the major said, rhetorically, it seemed to Jan.

Suddenly a loud scream could be heard, causing Jan to stiffen. The major ignored it, outwardly at least. Was it genuine, or had it been for his benefit? Sitting across from this Soviet officer, Jan remembered his joy at the arrival of the Soviet army in Prague, the Nazi prisoners they herded at the rear of their column. Jan had hoped to see Frank among them, but he must have escaped. It had seemed that his people's national nightmare was over, and the process of rebuilding their country would soon commence. The large Czech crowd had been jubilant, but Jan's father had been cautious, irrationally so in Jan's opinion.

"Do you like Katrina?" the major asked with a grin.

When Jan had told Drewniak about the singing he had heard that first night, his cagemate had suggested that the singer was a young woman. Was Katrina the huddled form he had seen several cages distant from his?

"Drewniak said there was a woman among us, but I have not actually seen her."

"Would you like to meet her?"

When Jan hesitated, the major said, "Consider it. You might be here for a while. Katrina could make your stay more bearable."

"I do not understand why I am being detained", Jan protested.

"I have been told you are an expert on detention sites."

"By whom? I know nothing about them, except what I have read and heard about the camps run by the Nazis ... and what I am now experiencing myself."

"What do you know of this place?"

"Drewniak told me it was an abattoir."

"A killing floor, yes. It was abandoned when we found it."

"May I ask what you intend to do with me?" Jan said, emboldened by the wine and the major's directness.

"You may ask, but I am not obliged to answer. There are ... discrepancies between the information I have received and what you have told me: troubling discrepancies." The major drained the dregs of wine from his glass and wiped his mouth with his sleeve. "Until these discrepancies are resolved, I cannot give you any guidance."

"Must I return to that cage?" Jan asked, knowing it sounded pitiful.

"Indeed."

Jan's heart fell. He knew it would do no good to plead with this man, and it might do harm. "Might I be provided with reading glasses and books while I am here?"

The major chuckled. "This is not a library." He tapped on the desktop and added, "I am afraid, Skala, that you have a mistaken notion of Soviet justice. Do you know that we are working to punish crimes against our brother countries, Czechoslovakia included?

"Let me tell you something. You do not know that the man your fellows call Herr Shithauler is Franz Heydrich, the uncle of the Butcher of Prague."

Jan was struggling to connect the little old man behind the cart with the bemedaled *Reichsprotektor* he had met one night in Prague. "Did he assist Heydrich or the Reich?" he asked the Russian.

"What does that matter? In fact, he was a librarian."

"Then why should I have a grievance with him?"

The major appeared to be astounded by Jan's question. "Did you not hear that the man's name is Heydrich and that he is a close relative of your mortal enemy?"

"Is that why he is here? Because he is a relative of an evil man, not because he himself is guilty of evil?"

"Yes, justice. Now listen to me. I want to inform you of something so that you do not try anything rash. You need not come to harm here. I am sure you noticed that there are alarms on all the cage doors. We know when any of them are opened: my own design, I am proud to say. So you see, even if you managed to open the door, and that is highly improbable, you would be found out immediately. I tell you this in a spirit of goodwill."

The major picked up the phone and said a few words in Russian into the receiver. Before Jan could think of a final word to say, the guard returned, took hold of one of Jan's arms, and escorted him out of the office. None too gently he urged Jan across the threshold and down the steps to the gravel yard.

A plane roared overhead. Reminded of the bombing and strafing he had witnessed in the war, Jan hesitated and looked up toward the clouds. "Move", the guard said, and he did.

November 4, 1945

Jan had filled the chamber pot to overflowing, and his bowels were still churning. He was so dehydrated that his tongue felt like dried leather, and his head pulsed with pain.

The bright cage-mounted lamps and windowless building made it impossible, unless the abattoir door was opened, to distinguish night from day. His scalp itched, and he wondered if it were infected or infested. He had no doubt that the army of creatures he couldn't see greatly outnumbered those that were visible. He remembered how Fran used to run her hands through his hair, and he imagined how messy he must look, how bad he must smell.

Night—or what passed for night in that place—consisted of maddeningly tedious hours and agonizing sensations. Jan knew that he had moaned loudly on several occasions and had cursed out loud more than once. There was constant music, loud music, accompanied by the snoring of the prisoners or their stirring: their occasional standing or sitting as the misery of reclining on the concrete floor or some mental terror compelled them to move. Because of his frequent need to empty his bowels, Jan had abandoned the warm floor pipes, and he was shivering uncontrollably by morning. Once his fitful sleep had been interrupted by the movement of something on his back. He had awakened to see a three-legged rat limping toward the fence. He hadn't bothered to strike out or even to shout; he had simply watched the creature as it sniffed the concrete floor and exited the cage.

"We had better hope it is the food and not cholera morbus", Schreiber said. "We shall know soon enough if it is cholera." As weary and worn as he was from that miserable night, Jan could not imagine hearing more terrifying words.

The young prisoner two cages away, attired in a gray sweater and brown corduroys, had climbed the fence to a height of about eight feet and was staring down at a huddled shape in a far cage.

"Katrina doesn't greet the new day until our gourmet breakfast is served," Drewniak said from behind him, "but have a good look. She doesn't seem to mind. Perhaps she likes it."

Jan resented the implication, but what was one more insult here?

Brandt, the Gestapo colonel, said, "I recognize that climbing pup: Klaus Fuch's student. How did he find his way to Germany ... and here? Don't be fooled by his silence. He speaks English, that one."

Drewniak, turning his back to Brandt, said, "Gestapo pig. I have personal knowledge of this reptile, and a worse scoundrel does not exist outside prison walls—or within them—than Brandt."

Jan glanced at Brandt, seeing the man's granite-like facial features, short blond hair, and those hard eyes that caused Jan to turn away, telling himself that he was fortunate to be in a cage with Drewniak, and not with Brandt as poor Schreiber was.

"What of your family, Skala?" Drewniak asked.

Jan remembered the major's cautionary statement about the Pole. "My father publishes a newspaper in Prague, or he once did. My mother left a long time ago. I have no brothers or sisters."

"Are you married?"

Jan shook his head.

"Is there a girl?"

"There *was*." How many times, day and night, had Jan thought of Fran since he was arrested?

"This ... um ... existence is easier if there are no attachments", said Drewniak in a way that made Jan wonder if he were speaking about their incarceration or about life in general.

The music was louder and even more discordant than usual. Brandt, standing in the center of his cage and speaking to no one in particular, boomed, "Might we have some Wagner instead of these tiresome Russians?"

The balding man in the red and white checked shirt, propped against the fence like a stuffed animal, responded, "Have you considered, dear Colonel, that you might never hear Wagner again?"

"Lutz would never say such a thing to Brandt if he were in Schreiber's place", Drewniak remarked. "These cages prevent us from escaping, and they prevent some of us from murdering others. This is no socialist paradise."

"Is that what you expected the Russians to bring?" Jan asked.

"Not paradise, perhaps, but somewhere a man might live and work in peace. I come from a big Catholic family, and I am the only one who survived the war. Look where faith in God has gotten Poland", he said. "I do not put much faith in man either, understand, because I know what to expect from him: damn little. And you? Have you any religion?"

Jan said, "My uncle is a cardinal."

"You are learning to deflect questions, a useful skill here. Is your uncle in Czechoslovakia, Rome?"

"Rome."

Drewniak said, "The Church is retreating to its Roman ghetto. I am surprised the Church has not collapsed along with everything else. Well, it is only a matter of time."

"You fought the Germans?" Jan asked Drewniak.

"I was in the Krakow resistance. One of the lucky ones who survived, if you can call this lucky. I might not be a good Catholic, but I am a patriot. I was detained by the Soviets when they liberated the city. They released me, but a few weeks ago they arrested me and brought me here."

A patriot: That was how Jan had described himself before, and to the major. "Why were you arrested?"

"Did they give *you* a reason? They say nothing, but we are all suspected of sedition."

Jan's mouth was so dry that it was difficult to speak, but now he was enraged. "How can they pen us up with pigs like Brandt? We resisted the Nazis."

"So you say. Our presence here suggests that the Russians are not convinced we are on their side."

"Then they are fools", Jan said bitterly.

"Powerful fools. I would choose my words more carefully if I were you", Drewniak whispered, tapping his lips with a finger. "I myself have a wife", Drewniak continued. "I have not seen her for almost a year, but I believe—I hope—she is still alive. Danuta is her name."

In a cage next to Jan's, the major's Charlie Chan was squatting in the corner as his cagemate, Nagy, was pacing frenetically. In the cage next to theirs, the thick-browed man in the red vest, Brio, sat on the concrete cross-legged, scratching on the floor with something. His cagemate, Otto Bache, though big of frame, looked like a walking corpse. His eyes popped from their sockets, one arm hung lifelessly, and he limped. Drewniak had told Jan that this man had supplied the Germans with arms.

Out of the corner of his eye, Jan saw one of the guards come into the building. This one, whose name was Fyodor, had dark hair and eyes and was missing part of an ear. He carried a lacquered black stick that he flipped in the air like a juggler. Fyodor was carrying his stick in one hand and a bucket in the other. Instinctively, everyone moved away from the fence: everyone except the young prisoner who had climbed the wire.

"That blockhead couldn't count to ten without his fingers. And that's no sure thing either, lads", Drewniak remarked loudly enough for those nearby to hear.

Fyodor, oblivious to the Pole's insult, went from cage to cage. Every time the guard unlocked a cage, a siren sounded for several seconds. Once inside the cage, Fyodor poured sloppy stew and deposited moldy bread into each prisoner's tin bowl. He hitched the stick to his belt but never took his eyes off the prisoners he was feeding.

When Fyodor reached the Chinese and Nagy's cage, Jan heard Drewniak whisper, "There is another guard with a rifle on the catwalk. He is covering Fyodor. These Russians know their business. Please do not do anything foolish. I might be in their line of fire."

Jan glanced up and saw the second guard. How had this man gotten into the building? He hadn't entered with Fyodor. Jan hadn't noticed him at prior meals. Indeed, Jan had been concocting a desperate idea to overcome Fyodor and make a dash for it. Had Drewniak read his mind? After a mere three days in this place, Jan admitted to himself, he was probably as transparent as a pane of glass.

The climber had not descended when Fyodor reached his cage, not even after Fyodor shouted, "Down, dog!" The guard nimbly scaled the outside of the cage and rapped on the man's knuckles with his stick. At first, the climber took no notice, but after a half-dozen blows he fell to the floor moaning. Fyodor then entered the cage, menacing the young man with his stick as he filled the bowls. All the while, the climber's cagemate, the old man, sat as still as a statue.

The next cage on Fyodor's circuit was Katrina's. She had gotten to her feet and was waiting for him. She wasn't a beauty, but even at a distance of thirty feet she exuded sensuality. In spite of himself, Jan was stirred. Fyodor leered at her as he filled her bowl. Before she began eating, she looked Jan full in the face and smiled at him.

By the time Fyodor reached his cage, Jan was eager for the meal, not caring that it was barely edible. Most of those who had been fed had already wolfed down their food, and it was all Jan could do not to emulate them, in spite of his malady that had probably been caused by spoiled food.

After Jan finished the sour-tasting mess, he went to the corner of the cage where he could see the woman better. She was standing on the side of her cage nearest his, oblivious to the young prisoner who had climbed the fence again and was looking down at her like a buzzard.

Jan saw a cat slink into the woman's cage and sit beside her. He forced himself to turn away. He was still hungry and thirsty, and he cringed inwardly at the thought that he wouldn't see food again for many hours.

The man in the cage with Lutz: What in the devil was he up to? It took Jan a few minutes to realize that the man, named Petrenko, was saying Mass. He must have saved a piece of bread, Jan thought. He needed bread, didn't he? Didn't he also need wine?

"Crazy", Drewniak said to Jan, nodding in the direction of the priest. "Perhaps that is too harsh a judgment. Petrenko is just a man, a frightened man, like the rest of us. If there is something we can cling to, perhaps we can retain our sanity."

When the priest completed the rite, he retired to the corner of the cage. Most of the prisoners settled into a passive state. Some slept. Others stared. Still others paced like caged animals.

Jan's single obsession was release—or escape. How could he discern what his captor wanted him to admit, but without attaching too much guilt to himself? The problem was that he didn't know what his captor wanted. The major was convinced of—or at least suspected—something.

It had been dangerous to be a journalist when the Germans arrived in Prague. Many of Jan's friends and coworkers fled the city before the Nazis got there, having heard that their names were on blacklists. Jan knew that if he remained, he would need to convince the Nazis of his sympathy, or at least of his willingness to cooperate. He could serve his country better by remaining, he had told himself. For the Nazis' part, they saw value in keeping Jan at the newspaper. They could make use of his knowledge, contacts, and language skills while maintaining the illusion of a "free press" that adhered to the official German narrative.

From the moment Jan agreed to work for Frank, he knew that he would be killed if he violated the man's directives. Were the Soviets going to be equally oppressive? Had one brutal overlord been replaced by another? He could barely stand to entertain such an idea, not after he and his countrymen had experienced the exhilaration of liberation from the Germans.

Was Jan's subservience to Frank when the Nazis had taken control of the newspaper the reason he was here?

"You must write that the rumors about Lidice are communist propaganda", Frank had said after the Germans, like mad hornets, had gone on a killing spree in retaliation for Heydrich's assassination.

"It is too late for that", Jan had replied, before considering his words.

36

"Do as you are told, Skala."

Jan knew better than to defy Frank when the German used this tone of voice. Jan remembered writing that the story of the Nazi massacre—of an entire village being wiped out—was a Russian fairy tale, fabricated to make the Germans look bad. Only those responsible for Heydrich's murder had been brought to justice.

What else could Jan have done? Could this be behind his incarceration: someone seeking revenge for Jan's perceived collaboration with the Germans?

How different those wartime days were from those when Jan had started working at the paper. He recalled the time Cermak, editing an article Jan had prepared about the death of a prominent Prague philanthropist, had replaced the dead man's name with that of a two-headed hound named Barnum and Bailey, an initiation that had caused Jan's colleague to roar with laughter when Jan was convinced that the article had gone to press.

The black and white cat, tail held high, was creeping along the wall. The music began blaring again, and someone—Jan thought it was Brandt—uttered a loud curse.

November 6, 1945

Jan was considering how to escape from the cage, and the abattoir. This was a makeshift prison; there must be a way out for a resourceful and determined man.

The cages were identical, about ten feet by ten feet square, with heavy-gauge chain-link fence on all four sides extending fifteen feet above the floor; not new material, but sturdy. The tops of the cages were open; the barbed wire was the impediment. Loops of spiked wire topped the entire perimeter of each cage, protruding several feet into the cage and out over the sides at the top, like a ring of icing on the top of a cake. A man would be cut to pieces if he tried to surmount it. At the bottoms of the cages, pins had been drilled into the concrete floor to secure the wire so that it couldn't be pried up, and the doors, equipped with built-in locks, were made of heavier wire than the cage itself.

"You cannot get out unless they let you out", Drewniak said, observing that Jan was studying his surroundings.

"Ha!" Brandt bellowed. "Do you call this a prison? Heinrich could teach these Russki goblins something. Heinrich trusted me. I never betrayed his trust, and I never shall."

Drewniak spat in Brandt's direction and said, "What I would not have given for a rifle and a locked room with you, Himmler, and your beloved Führer."

"Too late, *Panje*, and you do not have ... *die Nüsse* for the job."

Ignoring the two men, Jan looked up at the roof. The catwalk that passed over the top of Jan and Drewniak's cage might have been a hundred feet high, instead of its actual twenty feet. Could Jan disable the door alarm without triggering it by wrenching out the wire?

Even if he managed to escape from the cage, could he count on the others to keep silent? Surely someone would alert the guards to curry favor; only one would have to succumb to this temptation, and more than a few of these men were unreliable. Likewise, if he managed to overcome a guard, it was only too likely that another prisoner would raise the alarm.

Turning his attention back to Jan, Drewniak said, "There are too many eyes and ears in this place. You could not trust us. Escape is more than a matter of tactics."

That was what Karl Hermann Frank had been fond of saying: "This is more than a matter of tactics, Skala. You must make these people feel the way we want them to feel, not merely think the way we want them to think. In doing so, you will be doing them a service, preventing unnecessary casualties, keeping them alive."

SS-Obergruppenführer Frank had compelled him to editorialize against the Jews and the Church, and when Jan had tried to retain a shred of integrity, Frank had edited these phrases out with a stroke of his pen.

Like Frank, the Russian major saw through Jan; he would not let Jan rationalize his accommodation of the Germans.

"Damn them!" Jan said out loud.

"Yes, by all means", Drewniak said jovially.

Jan took hold of the fence and tried to shake it. The wire barely moved, and the noise he made was scarcely audible. If only he could make something like a rope and gain access to the catwalk. But what could he use to make rope, and how could such a project be kept secret?

Jan shook the fence again, but with less enthusiasm, admitting to himself that Drewniak was right. If he were to escape, it would have to be along much different lines than he was imagining.

He recalled the wire barriers he had seen in the catacombs while visiting his uncle in Rome. Years ago Jan's uncle, a newly minted bishop, had opened to Jan all the treasures of the Vatican. High summer, and Rome was hot and lazy; it was hard to imagine such a world in this bone-chilling prison.

Yet Jan's thoughts turned to his last summer with Frantiska. He could see her as she had been the night he had asked her to marry him. She had not said yes, but she had given him reason to hope.

Had she changed him, Jan wondered, or was he attributing more influence to her now than he had before his abduction? He knew that he had genuine affection for her, but had it ever been more than that? And how deep was her feeling for him? How assiduously was she searching for him? Surely, he told himself, Frantiska would not let him go that easily. She knew about Frank, but Jan had been ashamed to tell her more than what was necessary. When pro-German articles were published under his byline, he had denied authorship. But what could she do about his absence? What could anyone do in a country that had been stripped by the Nazis of all organs of justice?

Ever since he had arrived here, Jan could not think of Frantiska without recalling that night—it had been just one night—with her friend Anicka. He had known it was a mistake; he knew it as the night was progressing and knew it afterward. Frantiska had never learned of it; he was almost certain of that, but he had never been able to consign the memory—and he had tried very hard—to that of a rash and witless act. Why, he asked himself, did it gnaw on him so much more now?

Frank, in that droll yet menacing way of his, had let Jan know that he was aware of that night, giving the Nazi even more power over Jan than he had before.

The stomach distress Jan had experienced two days earlier had subsided; it had not gone away so much as diminished to fits of queasiness. He had even managed to sleep for longer than a few minutes at a time. Once he had been awakened by an animal howling, causing him to wonder if there were wolves in the area.

"Time for Mass yet, priest?" Nagy asked sarcastically. The Hungarian's gold-buttoned sweater and chocolate brown slacks were now caked with grime and cement dust.

Jan looked in the direction of the Petrenko-Lutz cage. Adolph Lutz was sitting with his back against the cage, and Ivan Petrenko was standing in the center of the cage with his eyes closed.

"Are you out of bread? Will this do?" Nagy raised the remains of a fish skull above his head. Some of the others laughed.

"Must you talk of food?" Daniel Brio interjected. "I cannot get a *foie gras en croute* out of my mind."

"I wish I could offer you some wine. I once had a decent cellar, but now all I have is this pot", said the Hungarian loutishly.

The music ceased. Lutz cupped his hands and shouted, "Tikhon Khrennikov has been censored!"

Nagy, apparently tired of taunting Petrenko, wandered to the other side of the cage. His cagemate, the Chinese dressed as a Russian soldier, was exercising, or dancing, in balletic, martial movements. When the man completed this activity, he walked to the corner of his cage and knelt over something.

It was still hours until the evening meal, and many of the prisoners were sleeping or subsisting in that state of half-consciousness they adopted as antidotes to boredom and sadness.

When the Chinese finished what he was doing, he approached Jan, who had been watching him, and said, "I am Chan Zemin."

So the major dubbing him Charlie Chan was more than a theatrical flourish. Few of the prisoners ever bothered to introduce themselves or even acknowledge other prisoners. Despite being in such close proximity to one another, isolation was the norm. Jan and Drewniak's laconic conversations could be considered garrulous in comparison to many cagemates, who went days without saying a word to each other.

"Jan Skala, from Prague."

The beardless Chan was pale and slight, the smallest of the prisoners except for Katrina, yet he seemed more virile than all the others, even the young climber.

"Where did you get this plant?" Jan asked him, glancing in the direction of the green sprout over which the Chinese had been kneeling.

"Weed grow from crack in floor. Guards not notice."

"How do you keep it alive?"

"Chamber pot good for more than one thing", Chan said, grinning.

Jan glanced at the pitiful weed. "Where did you learn English?"

"Studied Russian and English in Shanghai. Taught Confucian way as a boy, but life in China make me think Russians discover better way. Realize error too late. Russian way no better than Chinese way. When I leave Soviet army, am charged with treason."

Suddenly, a loud voice, a performing voice, erupted with:

What are the roots that clutch, what branches grow
Out of this stony rubbish? Son of man,
You cannot say, or guess, for you know only
A heap of broken images, where the sun beats,
And the dead trees give no shelter, the cricket no relief,
And the dry stone no sound of water.

Jan recognized Eliot's poem from his days in England.

Brio's oration was interrupted more than once by Brandt, who made insulting remarks, and by Nagy, who said, "Has he gone mad?"

"He is reciting verse!" Lutz shouted back from an adjacent cage.

"You think Fyodor's stick knows the difference?" Nagy barked.

Daniel Brio went on as if he were oblivious to his fellow prisoners:

The shouting and the crying.
Prison and place and reverberation
Of thunder of spring over distant mountains.
He who was living is now dead.
We who were living are now dying.

Brio used his dirty sweater sleeve to mop his face as if he had been engaging in hard labor. Someone clapped perfunctorily, maybe sarcastically.

"Do the Soviets have the numbers to stay in Germany ... Czechoslovakia?" Jan asked Drewniak.

"The answers to such questions cannot be reduced to numbers", Drewniak responded warily.

43

Werner Schreiber, with his face pressed against the fence, said, "There is nothing in this world that cannot be reduced to numbers."

One thousand, four hundred twenty-two Czechs were murdered in Allied bombing raids in the past week. These "liberators" are killing Czechs and destroying our heritage. Such lies had Jan been compelled to write.

"You are wrong about that, friend", Lutz said, pulling himself from the floor by grasping the fence, revealing a large hole in the elbow of his sweater. "Put dogma in the dustbin, but do not make me a slave to numbers. Take James ... his will to believe. Do not mistake his beliefs"—he gave Ivan Petrenko a hard look—"for those of these fools. It is not that at all. For James, experience reveals truth."

Jan was only listening with half an ear, wondering what truth had to do with the number of men the Soviets needed to subdue Germany, or Czechoslovakia.

"You are a physicist. How can you say such things?" Schreiber asked Lutz scornfully, glancing nervously at a prone Brandt in the corner of their cage. "How does James measure truth?"

"We experience the divine, the supreme reality. This is a real effect. I can explain better in German ... but the guards' sticks.... For James the higher part of the universe—not the god of this priest—is real."

"Spare us this ... speechifying, for God's sake", Nagy moaned.

"Give me an example of what you are talking about", Schreiber demanded, ignoring Nagy.

"Music!" Lutz exclaimed.

"Not so loud," Drewniak said, "or someone might uncensor that awful Russian composer. What was his name, Lutz?"

"Khrennikov."

Jan was not convinced that music proved anything. During the occupation, he remembered, Frank required that the Prague Opera continue to perform, that is, after all those of Jewish or so-called Gypsy extraction had been removed from the orchestra and replaced by those of Aryan stock. Frank selected the repertoire and patronized the performances. He ordered Jan to accompany him on several occasions to reinforce Jan's connection to the German program. As

Jan was leaving the opera house with Frank one evening, he recalled with distress, someone had spat on him.

Schreiber shook his head and said, "Even music is mathematical."

Lutz, clutching the fence, said, "Music is more than that! It speaks to us of things that cannot be put into words, never mind numbers."

The priest had been watching and listening, his eyes shifting from Lutz to Schreiber as they talked. At last he said, "Music ... *good* music, is beauty. Beauty is more than numbers. Beauty is ... a person."

"The same person who lives in your crust of bread, I suppose", said Lutz.

Brio, who had been sitting with his head cupped in his hands ever since he finished his verses, looked up and said, "I am with Schreiber. Beauty delights me also, but this is only sensation, nothing more."

"Happiness is ... sensation?" Petrenko asked.

"Of course!" Lutz said. "Open your eyes, man. Look around you. Can you be happy here? In hunger, in pain ... robbed of your freedom? What is necessary is ... *accommodation*."

Yes, Jan said to himself, accommodation is the necessary thing. He could see that this conversation was taking its toll, though these men had barely moved. Petrenko could hardly stand. Both Lutz and Schreiber were now sitting on the concrete floor. During a lull in the conversation, when one man was catching his breath and another steadying himself, it came to Jan, as to one looking into a previously murky pool in which all of the sediment had now settled, that none of these men were ordinary political prisoners. They were educated, cultured. Schreiber had identified Lutz as a physicist. Many spoke fluent English. They must be here for a reason and maybe were together for a reason.

"Aristotle says that happiness is not a state of being", Petrenko said, "or an *accommodation*, as you put it, but an *activity*. A man might be happier in this prison than walking the streets of ... Vienna."

"I prefer 'way station' to 'prison'", Drewniak quipped.

Drewniak too, Jan thought. Drewniak was special too.

"I will take my chances in Innsbruck", piped Lutz, picking something out of his scalp, "*mit einer Fräulein auf meinem Arm. Now look what you have made me say.*"

45

"Damn you!" Nagy bellowed. "My head is going to split open."

Drewniak said, "Keep talking, lads, and let us test Nagy's prediction."

Out of the corner of his eye, Jan saw Fyodor walk purposefully into the building. It wasn't mealtime, and he was followed by the guards Piotr and Evgeny. Fyodor and Evgeny's sticks were prominently displayed, while Piotr bore a rifle. Evgeny, less frequently in the building than the other two, was short and squat, with yellow hair, legs like tree stumps, and sky-blue eyes. Evgeny was a head shorter than Fyodor and two heads shorter than Piotr. He knew little English, just a few words of command and derision.

Lutz moaned audibly and crouched in a corner of his cage.

The fence climber, who often defied the guards by shaking the cage or howling at them, retreated as far from his door as possible. Jan sensed something was about to happen, but he was not sure what that might be.

The guards walked briskly past Brio and Bache, Chan and Nagy; then they turned left, past Petrenko and Lutz, stopping at Schreiber and Brandt's cage. Fyodor inserted a key in the lock, the door rattled open, and the alarm sounded. Werner Schreiber had backed up to the opposite side of the cage. None of the other prisoners made a sound. Brandt had been sleeping and was now lurching to his feet.

"Come", Evgeny said to Brandt, waving his stick.

Like a flame behind a frosted window, fear flickered across Brandt's face. The expression faded in an instant, and Brandt's nostrils flared. He stiffened his spine and stepped forward as if he were entering a parade ground.

Evgeny raised his stick, and Piotr covered Brandt with the gun, but as if these were unnecessary inducements, the German calmly exited the cage. Fyodor slammed the door and locked it, a kind of exclamation point that released the prisoners' tension: the guards had not come for them, not today, not yet. As Brandt left the building he shouted, "Heil Hitler!"

A few minutes later, the prisoners heard the report of several rifles being fired at once, followed by one additional shot.

"For good measure", Drewniak said to no one in particular.

A rat that had been lurking in the shadows near the boiler darted between the cages, and Jan recalled a vivid dream from the previous night: the abattoir trenches were filled with blood, with rats swimming like fish in the crimson liquid, sometimes paddling, sometimes diving and disappearing from sight.

For the first time, Jan had witnessed a prisoner being led to his execution, and his mind was already occupied with rationalizing why Brandt had been chosen and why he had no reason to fear the Nazi's fate.

Knowing the prisoners' disdain for Brandt, Jan was surprised that some of them—Schreiber and Nagy in particular—had not cheered or applauded his death. Instead they had slumped to the floor of their cages without a word.

The prisoners' routine went on as usual, as if nothing untoward had happened that day. Old Heydrich, accompanied by Piotr, came to empty the pots, but he ran his cart into a curb, causing the half-filled drum to slide onto the floor. It was about to tip over when the bull-like Piotr lifted the heavy drum and replaced it on the cart.

"The girl likes you", Drewniak said to Jan. "She is interested in one of us, and she never paid attention to me before you arrived."

"She is desperate", Jan said. "We are all desperate."

"Have it your own way", Drewniak answered. "Some of these ... ah ... deprived fellows would kill to be her favorite."

Jan was sure that Drewniak was right about the other prisoners. He walked to the fence, and Katrina got up from the floor and came to the side of her cage nearest Jan. He sensed that many eyes were now looking at him, at them.

Schreiber ambled toward Jan's cage and said, "You have made a friend, I see."

Jan didn't answer. It was none of Schreiber's business, or Drewniak's for that matter. Now in a cage by himself, Schreiber, a small studious sort of man in his fifties, looked jauntier than before.

Numbers, Jan told himself. Two minus one equals contentment, at least what passed for contentment here.

47

"I will not miss the Nazi. He was objectionable in every way", Schreiber said to Jan, as if reading condemnation in his expression. "I am a professor of economics. Brandt and his comrades did not like my ideas, *und* so they sent me to a camp near Sachsenhausen. Of course—as you can see—the Soviets do not like me either."

"You seem to know why you are here", Jan said.

"The Russians control much of Germany now, and Poland, and Czechoslovakia. Do you need to know more than that?"

"What is that supposed to mean?" Brio interjected. "Marxists look out for the proletariat, the working man and woman."

"That is a quaint idea," Petrenko's raspy voice intruded, "but my experience contradicts this. In Ukraine, where I am from, many working men and women have been starved and murdered by the Bolsheviks."

Jan began to circle the cage, walking until his legs began to cramp, remembering the dream about the swimming rats, remembering Brandt marching out the door, remembering the smirking faces of Frank and the major.

Where was his father? The major had suggested that his father had fled Prague. And to where? A mountain retreat, Austria, Italy, and the protection of Jan's uncle? Jan's family had been well connected before the war destroyed, or redistributed, wealth, status, and privilege. Now where could his father turn for succor? If his father was in peril, was it because of Jan's complicity with the Nazi program?

Jan might not have been a hero, he told himself, but he wasn't a villain either. Others had retreated to the wilderness, bombed and killed the Germans, but who was to say they were the greater patriots? What happened after these heroes assassinated Heydrich? Lidice, that's what happened. Yet the men who brought that upon their countrymen were now wearing ribbons, while he was without his liberty, in mortal danger.

More questions without answers, more trouble than a man ought to bear. He crawled to the pipes and slept.

November 10, 1945

Piotr made his way slowly to Jan and Drewniak's cage. The guard unlocked the cage and motioned with his stick for Jan to exit. He made Jan walk in front. No one said anything, not even Drewniak. Jan fought back the vertiginous sensation that accompanied an image of Brandt being led to his execution and concentrated on putting one foot in front of the other.

Outside the building, a cold wind pierced through Jan's clothes. Though pale and cloudless, the sky, which he had not seen for days, dazzled him. Piotr gave Jan a prodding rap with his stick to hurry him along. They detoured around a swath of gravel black with oil and had almost reached the office when Piotr whispered, "Be careful."

These words puzzled Jan. Why would Piotr warn him? Or was the sadistic guard trying to evoke fear? That made more sense. In any event, Jan didn't need to be warned to be on his guard.

The major sat behind his desk as before. The Russian was leaning forward with his fingertips pressing down upon the desktop like a cat preparing to pounce upon its prey.

"How are you getting along with Charlie?" the major asked.

It took a moment for Jan to recall that "Charlie" was Chan Zemin. "An interesting man", Jan said cautiously.

The major raised his right index finger. "And a deserter."

Jan knew that it would be perilous to indulge his inclination to defend Chan. At their first meeting, Jan had hoped to convince the major to release him. Now he knew that a different approach was necessary—but what?

Jan stared at the desk, as if the answer were engraved in the wood. Frank had also questioned him from behind a desk, the one once occupied by Jan's editor. The editor and many of Jan's colleagues had fled or gone underground before the Nazis arrived. The Writer's Café, where they would gather after putting the newspaper to bed, became an all-but-empty shell during the occupation, because it was known that the café was being watched by the Gestapo.

"You have gotten to know Drewniak better, I presume?"

Another tactic to pry Jan open: How could he have avoided getting to know the Pole better, living together as they were in a small cage?

"He pretends to be a good socialist", the Russian said, taking a moment to light a cigarette and inhale. "He pretends to be a man of principle. He is neither."

"I only know what he has told me", Jan said.

"And what has Drewniak told you?"

"He told me he fought the Nazis, that he is a socialist."

"He would say so", the major exclaimed with some vehemence. "That man is a liar."

"What is he, then, if not what he claims to be?"

"Now you interrogate me. And I will answer you. Drewniak is the sort of patriot who interferes with the new, the necessary, order. He would resist the inevitable."

"What is inevitable?"

"That should be obvious: European socialism."

"You have the advantage of me. I know very little about Drewniak."

"A man like Drewniak can get you into trouble", the major said. "Trust me."

"Then might I be moved out of that building?"

"I have already offered to move you."

Jan knew the major was referring to Katrina, but if he agreed to be moved into the cage with Katrina, wouldn't the other prisoners conclude he was a Russian informer?

"Have you seen much of the beautiful Katrina?" the major continued.

How could Jan avoid seeing her, looking at her, thinking about her?

"Would you like to get to know her better?"

"Yes", Jan said, hoping that by cooperating with the major he could earn his release or at least be moved out of the abattoir.

The major drew on his cigarette several times. He never took his eyes off Jan. "We are having a visitor. He has asked to speak with you", he said.

Chan, Drewniak, Katrina, and now this visitor. What was the man up to?

The Russian put down his cigarette and, speaking in a confidential tone, said, "It is in *your* interest to cooperate."

"What would you have me say?"

"Why, the truth, by all means: that you are being treated well, that you are part of a . . . ah . . . legitimate investigation. That's all."

Jan could not stifle a sad grin.

"Here, listen well, Skala." It was the first time the major had said his name. "It will go badly for you if this visitor makes trouble. You will gain nothing. He cannot free you. Only I can free you. Do not dare to make an enemy of me. Understand?"

Jan looked into those steely eyes and nodded.

"Good. This visitor will be here in three days. That will give you time to reflect, to prepare yourself. Of course, everything you say and do when you meet this man will be heard and observed. Even a . . . ah—"

"Subtle sign?"

"Yes, even a subtle sign will be recognized by us."

Everything you say and do when you meet this man will be heard and observed. So it had been when Jan met his friend at the Writer's Café, the quiet and mild-mannered fellow Jan had never thought of as a man of action. Thus, Jan was shocked when the man had said, "We want you to help us to eliminate Frank." At first Jan thought that his friend was making a bad joke, or perhaps the man had suffered a mental collapse. Didn't the fool realize that the café was being watched?

"I see that you are accommodating the new reality", said the major, interrupting Jan's thoughts. "That is essential for survival. Are you warm enough?"

"Yes."

"Would you like a glass of wine?"

"Yes. Thank you."

The major brought forth a new bottle of wine from behind the big desk. He took his time opening the bottle and poured two generous glasses, tumblers from his drawer. He handed one to Jan and tapped the glass with his own.

"To a pleasant Prague evening ... in future."

We will supply the bomb, but we need someone to attach the device to the underside of Frank's desk. We will detonate the bomb from the street. You need not be in the building. No one will suspect you.

After taking a sip of wine, the major continued, "I have Marshal Zhukov to thank for these bottles from Goering's cellar. Georgy Konstantinovich is a family friend."

Jan knew of Zhukov, that fearless and relentless warrior who had driven Hitler's armies from Leningrad, Stalingrad, and Moscow. If Zhukov was the major's patron, then his captor could act with impunity. Was that the message this man wanted to convey?

"Cigarette?" asked the major, lighting another for himself. "My mistake—I forgot that you do not smoke."

Holding his cigarette in one hand and the glass of wine in the other, the major said, "Our visitor is a British lawyer and army officer. He is a Labour man not unsympathetic to European socialism."

Jan was unable to restrain himself any longer. "What must I do to be set free?"

"How direct you are. Yet I have reason to believe you have not been perfectly candid with me."

Jan's heart fell, but he was determined to persist. "In what respect?"

The major had taken another sip of wine and was letting it linger in his mouth. He swallowed and said, "How do you like the wine?"

Jan noticed that his glass was almost empty. He hadn't realized he had imbibed so greedily. "It's very good", he said. It was not lost on Jan that the major hadn't answered his question.

"What must I do to be set free?" Jan repeated, this time in Russian.

The major poured a dash of wine into Jan's glass. Jan tried to restrain himself from consuming it in one gulp, but the deprivations of the abattoir made him so greedy that such self-control required herculean effort.

"I have told you that speaking in a language other than English is prohibited", said the major, putting the bottle away. "I will overlook your transgression this time, but not again. Now, where is your father?"

"I do not know", Jan answered, stung by his captor's strong rebuke.

"I am sorry to say that this is a bad start if you wish to be released."

Jan suspected that everything else had been a prelude to this line of questioning. He said in reply, "If I truly do not know where he is, I could fabricate an answer, or I could tell you the truth. I choose to tell you the truth: I do not know."

"I am almost inclined to believe you", the major said, lighting still another cigarette. "Where might he have gone?"

This was an even more dangerous question. Even though Jan did not know his father's whereabouts, to provide the major with places and names was a kind of betrayal.

Betrayal: Jan had been terrified by his friend's proposal in the café. Of course, the Nazis would suspect him because few were permitted in Frank's office. By no means would he ever consider such a thing. His friend must refrain from contacting Jan in the future. Jan had struggled for weeks with the decision about whether he should inform Frank, even wondering if this were a test by the Gestapo. He had decided to keep quiet, telling himself he was doing his patriotic duty by protecting his friend from the consequences of this absurd scheme.

The Russian was watching Jan with a knowing expression that terrified him. "He might have gone to Rome," Jan began, "the Vatican. His brother—my uncle—is in residence there."

"I do not think so. The road from Prague to Rome is being watched. And I do not think you think so either. Where else might he have gone?"

So far, Jan had given nothing away that the Russian didn't already know. He said, "My father has always enjoyed the mountains. He has friends there." This was a lie, and he wondered if he could sustain it.

"Who are they? Where are they?"

"I do not know the family names", Jan temporized. "Childhood friends of my father's. Karl is one, I think, and Liberec is the town."

"I see. Where else might he have gone?"

"Have you searched Prague? He might be there."

The major crushed his cigarette in the ashtray. "We do not think so," he said, eyes flashing, "but you are a convincing liar."

"I am not lying."

"We shall see. Let us talk about your collaboration with the Nazis."

"I resisted the Germans without giving them cause to kill me. I was not active in the Czech underground, if that is what you are asking. There are other ways to resist."

"How does giving in to Gestapo pressure to write exactly what they tell you to write meet the definition of resistance?"

Jan started and said, "What do you mean?"

The major wagged his stubby index finger and said, "You know exactly what I mean. When the Gestapo told you to write something, you did so."

Jan's cooperation with the Nazis, or so he insisted to himself, had never been as cowardly, as sordid, as his captor made it out to be, but it had been a source of shame to Jan that he had to take direction from Frank. "I had to make a choice: Accept the Nazi bridle or be executed . . . and abandon my countrymen."

"Is your father close to his brother, the cardinal?" the Russian asked.

"My father is not a religious man."

"So I have been told, but men are not always what they appear to be. The last time we met, I asked you about Lev Bronstein. Did any of the Trotskyites ever ask you to convey something for them?"

"Like what?" Jan asked and immediately regretted it.

"Answer my question, but be careful. Do not attempt to deceive me."

54

Be careful. That was what Piotr had told him. Jan said, "I do not associate with any Trotskyites, to the best of my knowledge, and I have not conveyed anything for anyone ... not that I can remember."

The major stared at Jan with the impervious expression of a basilisk. "Perhaps you possess something, or have passed it on to another party, that ought to be revealed to me."

"Something?" Jan asked, seeking a clue.

"Nothing comes to mind?"

"I am sorry ... nothing."

The Russian put a freshly-lit cigarette down on the edge of the ashtray, changed his mind, threw it on the floor, and stamped it out with his boot while still sitting. Then he turned both palms upward and said, "How can I help you if you will not help me?"

Jan could hear a low-flying plane, though the windows were closed. The Russian was clean and tidy, while he was filthy, lice infested. His stomach had started hurting again. He hadn't gone a day since he had arrived at this camp without experiencing agonizing stomach cramps.

"Who is your ... I believe the English word is *control*?"

"I do not understand."

"Control."

Jan shook his head vigorously.

The Russian shouted the word, this time in Czech.

Hearing his native language so startled Jan that he almost responded in the same tongue, but he composed himself and said, "I still do not understand."

"A worthy performance. I want to know the name of your control. Tell me, give me a name, and you may go home—today."

Jan's frustration boiled over, vying with utter exhaustion, erupting with, "Will you tell me what you think I have?" The wine had not stupefied him, but in his deprived state the alcohol had overstimulated him. He stood unsteadily, experiencing a sharp pain in his abdomen, but then, seeing the major's cautionary look and the man's right hand disappear below the desktop, Jan sat down again.

A minute might have passed before the major said, "You should know that we know everything that happens in the abattoir—day and night; you should know that there is no escape from this place; you should know that the only way out is for me to release you. Escape, British lawyers, pleas from your countrymen: none of these can help you. Think about this. My patience is not limitless. Do you understand?"

"Yes", Jan said resignedly.

"We shall see." The Russian reached below the desktop, and Piotr entered the office.

"You may go", Jan's captor said.

The abattoir was still, and Jan was prone on the floor of his cage, thinking about the major's keen interest in his father. Jan could not predict where that man was or what he might be doing. He heard himself telling his father, "Frank is a brute."

"I have heard it on good authority that the Germans cannot hold out for long", his father had replied.

"Who told you this?"

"Never mind. The Germans would not tolerate my presence at the newspaper, but I am glad you are still there. Do not do anything stupid."

"What do you mean?"

"I mean crossing Frank or attempting to resign. That one will kill you in an instant. There are dozens of ways to be a devil, and Frank knows all of them; desperation will make him an even dirtier dog. He might try to kill both of us at the end, so be prepared to flee. I am surprised they have let me live."

"Why have they done so?" Jan had inquired.

"I have made myself *useful*, as have you. We are unconventional patriots."

Jan had not been able to tell if his father, that inscrutable man, was being serious.

"I am being watched. You may assume you are being watched too."

56

Jan had asked his father, "What are you seeking ... survival?"

"Bah! I want my newspaper back, and I want you with me. I will do anything to have my newspaper back. Believe me, I have already done things I could never have imagined myself capable of doing.

"You are looking at me strangely. I told you what I want. Mind your behavior with that German and be prepared to bolt like a rabbit. Have no shame in doing this. Which reminds me, in Prague sycophants breed like rabbits, so keep this conversation to yourself. Do not even tell Frantiska, understand?"

The Russians came, and the Germans went, and Jan's father went too, but where, and why?

November 13, 1945

Since Jan's recent interrogation by the major, Drewniak's aversion to talking to him had been obvious, and the nearer prisoners, except for Petrenko and Chan, had been reticent to engage him. Even Nagy's outbursts had been curtailed.

Ivan Petrenko didn't turn his back when Jan approached. Instead, the increasingly cadaverous-looking prisoner spoke to him, saying, "Our captor uses words as weapons."

"Has he ... interviewed you too?"

"Yes."

Petrenko's cheekbones were visible beneath his thin, stretched skin. His graying hair lapped his shirt collar. "As you say, he uses words to inflict fear and pain", Jan said softly.

"I suppose it is necessary in his line of work. I heard you say your uncle is a cardinal. Where is he?"

"Rome."

"Not a bad place to be", Petrenko replied.

"Rome saw its share of misery in the war", Jan observed.

"I am talking about the *peacetime* reality. Unless I am mistaken, the liberation of Rome and the *liberation* of Ukraine—and of your country too—will not be the same. In Rome, people may speak freely again, but not where these Russians leave their footprints. In some places words are still very dangerous things.... Control words, and minds can be controlled."

"The Church knows something about control", Jan countered.

"At times the Church has overstepped her bounds, but she knows better than anyone that the word ought to be a proposal to man ... a proposal, not something imposed on him."

"I am not familiar with a Church that proposes", said Jan, wondering if he could trust this man. Was Petrenko, or anyone else in this place, who he pretended to be?

"A cardinal and an anticardinal in one family", Drewniak observed, apparently enjoying the exchange.

"The Church's true mission is to offer forgiveness", Petrenko said. "Try to find mercy anywhere else, Jan Skala."

That was when Piotr entered the abattoir, with his stick at the ready, and escorted Jan out of the building.

When Jan awoke the next morning, it was almost as if the past twelve days had been an awful dream. He could almost imagine that he had been transmogrified from man to beast and back again.

He was lying in a bed with a pillow, a sheet, and a blanket. Light cascaded into the room from a window, a clean window, and a radiator warmed the room. He was warm and blessedly comfortable.

A small table stood next to the bed, and on top of it were a pitcher of water and two glasses along with a pack of cigarettes and a deck of playing cards. To the right of the bed was a water closet with a cramped but adequate tub. Jan had taken a warm bath before sleeping, observing more than one insect being conveyed by the dirty water into the drain. He had been provided with pajamas, of all things, and medication for the lice on his scalp, though he suspected the salve was intended to curtail his scratching rather than eradicate the vermin.

What had happened to his own home? Had the Russians confiscated it? Had it been ransacked? Even in the darkest days of the war, his home had been an oasis. To the best of Jan's knowledge, neither Frank nor the Nazis had ever crossed that threshold, nor had Jan given them cause to do so. Now, when he thought of that place, he felt like a man who had lost a priceless coin down a sewer, despondent of ever finding it again.

He was sitting on the bed with both feet on the floor when he heard a key in the lock. The door opened wide, and the major stepped into the room. "See," he said, "we are not inhuman when you cooperate." This was the first time Jan had seen the major on his feet. The Russian possessed a squat, toad-like lower body complementing his facial features; he waddled rather than walked. Not waiting for Jan to respond, the major looked around the room and said curtly, "Get dressed. You will have a visitor shortly."

Jan walked to the closet, where he found a clean white shirt, trousers, and polished black shoes. As he began to dress, the major continued, "As I told you before, this visitor is a British lawyer and army officer. His name is Colonel David Ben. He happens to be a—" The Russian smirked rather than finishing his thought.

A Jew, Jan thought to himself, a British Jew, and an army officer. Jan had written what Frank had made him write, but could he count on others to understand this? Could this visitor have seen articles he had written?

"You will tell Colonel Ben how humanely you are being treated", said the Russian, who paused and added, "Do not communicate anything like outrage to this man. It will not set you free; it will result in ... sadness, suffering. Remember that we will be watching and listening to everything."

"What do you want me to tell him?"

"The truth, of course: that you are being treated well. We have gone over this before. I am sure I can depend on you. Now shave and wash your face." The major turned and departed, closing the door behind him.

While shaving, Jan took stock of himself in the mirror. Though still in his thirties, his sunken eyes made him look older. His face was pallid, and his straight wheat-colored hair was longer than he could ever remember it being.

Jan tied his shoes and walked to the window. There was no one in the yard. In the distance, he could see scattered houses. To the left were empty pens next to a railroad spur, and in the corner of the property was a fenced stockade. As Jan gazed at the debris and litter on the ground, he pondered what his captor had told him. He was going to be interviewed by an Englishman, a lawyer, and he was expected to behave. If he didn't behave, he would be punished, maybe executed. Was there anything to be done except to acquiesce to the major's command?

Jan looked around the room and didn't see any surveillance devices, but he wasn't an expert at such things. In the desk there was nothing to write with or on. No note could be passed to the Englishman. If Jan had known Morse code, perhaps he could have blinked a message in English: l–i–e–s. Whatever he did, if he did anything at all, would have to be subtle. The problem was that anything subtle enough to fool his captors might also be missed by the visitor.

The major hadn't told him when the interview would take place, only that Jan needed to be well groomed and circumspect. How soon after the interview would he be returned to the cage? Or would they allow him to remain in the place he had spent the night if he put on a good performance, as Frank had allowed him to continue working at the newspaper?

Whatever suspicions Drewniak and the others harbored about him would only be aggravated by his newest absence from the prison. As Jan's mind darted from subject to subject, the Englishman was escorted into the room by Piotr. There had been no knock on the door, just the sound of the key in the lock followed by a creaking hinge.

Having groomed and dressed himself as the major had instructed, and notwithstanding his hollow eyes and borderline emaciation, Jan made a presentable enough figure. He realized that as a stranger to the man, his gauntness might be taken as having been produced by the ravages of war and not by his treatment at the hands of the Russians.

Piotr made the slightest bow as he backed out of the room and closed the door. The Englishman placed his black leather attaché next to the door and extended a hand. The visitor's grip was tentative.

"How do you do?" the man said. "As you probably know, I am Colonel David Ben, and I am representing the British government."

Jan nodded at the man and motioned to an empty chair. He pulled up the desk chair, and both men sat down, facing each other.

The Englishman had florid features and a long grainy neck like a stalk of white asparagus, which protruded from his oversize collar.

Jan guessed that he was in his forties. As soon as the visitor spoke, Jan noticed his crooked teeth.

"I was told you studied in England", the man said with some enthusiasm.

"I was at Cambridge for a year studying English literature."

"I am an Oxford man myself, but I won't hold it against you", the Englishman said blithely. Ben looked around the room. "I understand you live in Prague. Lovely city."

"It was."

"Ah, yes. The Americans bombed Prague, and I have heard it was a mistake. Those bombs were intended for Dresden, you see. War is damned ugly business, but Churchill did what was necessary to bring Hitler to his knees."

"Have you met Churchill?" Jan asked.

"Yes, to be sure. We belong to different political camps. You might not know that Churchill has been voted out of office. My people now lead the government."

Jan nodded. The major had said that the visitor was a member of the Labour Party.

"Churchill is a bull in a china shop, you know. That sort of man was needed to defeat the Nazis, but Britain and Europe are better off for his departure from the public stage now that hostilities have ceased." Ben raised both index fingers and added, "Attlee is better medicine for what ails Britain and Europe now."

Jan could only guess what "better medicine" meant to this man, but he knew not to ask the question. He forced an amicable smile.

"Do you know why I am here?" Ben asked.

Careful, Jan told himself. "I was told that you wanted to question me."

"I am here to learn how you are being treated. There is a certain amount of sharp practice in every government, especially with this bloody war, but His Majesty's government is averse to sharp practice becoming gross injustice."

Jan stared at the man. Would his visitor understand that what he would say next would be a lie? "I am well, as you can see", Jan said.

"Being detained is troubling, but the Russians have not mistreated me."

"Your English is good, more than the product of one year in England."

"Thank you. Languages are my specialty."

The visitor's chin descended slightly. "We have asked the Soviets to allow us to inspect these ... irregular facilities. I am acquainted with President Beneš and Foreign Minister Masaryk. As you might know, they lived in England during the war, and I had the pleasure of meeting them in London and at your president's residence in Buckinghamshire. Good fellows", Ben added cautiously.

"I spoke to the Foreign Minister recently ... in Prague", Jan said.

"He is well, I trust."

Less than a month before he was abducted, Jan had interviewed Masaryk. Though the foreign minister had done his best to affirm the sound relationship between his country and the Soviets, there had been an undercurrent of anxiety on Masaryk's part that no amount of prodding had convinced Masaryk to put into words. In fact, the more Jan pressed, the more Masaryk resorted to diplomatic speech. Later, Jan could not help wondering if Masaryk's reticence had been connected to the Soviets or to something he had heard about Jan.

"Why are you being detained?" Ben asked abruptly.

Jan had anticipated this question and had decided to be direct. "The Soviets suspect me of sedition."

"Sedition? What are you supposed to have done?"

"That question is better asked of the major."

"You must know what they suspect."

"You could say that everyone who survived the Nazi occupation is suspected of something. I am the first to admit I am not a hero."

"What did you do during the war?"

"I was a journalist for a Prague newspaper."

Ben stared hard at him and said, "I see."

Surely this man had been told what Jan had done during the war.

Ben produced a notebook and pen. "Very well. How long have you been here?" The Englishman was sitting as straight as a rod, speaking with a well-modulated Etonian accent. He was a perfect representation of Jan's image of the British upper class.

"Twelve days."

"How long do you expect to be ... detained?"

Jan put his hands together, saying, "Only until the Soviets confirm my innocence."

"Were you in the Czech resistance movement?"

Jan's heart beat faster. Was there no relief from this relentless question? England was never occupied by the Nazis. What did this man know about the choices Jan had to make? He watched Ben carefully for a sign that this man was familiar with his wartime articles. If so, the Englishman hid it expertly. Knowing that the major was listening, Jan said, "Yes, I resisted the Germans ... to the best of my ability."

"Admirable, I am sure", said the colonel, but Jan sensed these words were less than sincere, or was his own insincerity responsible for this perception?

"Is someone representing you?" Ben asked.

Another dangerous question. "Of course." Another lie.

"Are you able to communicate with your legal representative?"

Jan nodded.

"Russian ... Czech?"

"Czech ... in Prague. An able man."

"Very good. Is there anything I can do for you?"

If Ben believed what Jan was telling him, then Jan could only conclude that this Englishman was a fool, perhaps a well-meaning fool, but a fool nonetheless. During his time in England, Jan had met Labour Party members who were enamored with the Soviets and the vision of a workers' paradise. If Jan could be said to have a political philosophy, it was that people like himself should be able to pursue their interests without government interference. As to the working class, they required direction and discipline so that society functioned properly: essentially his father's philosophy if he had been honest with himself. He didn't argue with friends and acquaintances who embraced socialism, though he considered his own views superior to socialism and other popular movements. Upon the Russians' arrival in Prague, Jan had accepted the new occupiers, not because he had communist sympathies but because the country needed a stabilizing influence to prevent lawlessness and chaos.

Now Jan's heart sank, and the apprehension he had been feeling was supplanted by despondency. Cues and signals would be wasted on this man. The Russians, in a position of strength, had only agreed to this interview because it suited their propaganda needs.

Now the Englishman was writing with vigor. Ben looked up suddenly and said, "I understand there are other prisoners here. Are they also well treated?"

"All of them", Jan said without hesitation.

"Are there any English or French prisoners in this pris ... at this location?"

Though posed nonchalantly, the question was perilous. Was it the cynicism in which he was now steeped that caused Jan to consider if this were the only important question Ben had been sent here to ask? Thinking about Brio, Jan said, "No."

"No one?"

"No."

Ben circled several words on his notepad, lifted his pen, and said, "Has your family been notified of your whereabouts and ... situation?"

Was Ben offering to act as a liaison with Jan's family? He did not dare tell this man that the major would be delighted to learn where his father was. Perhaps, Jan considered, David Ben had been prompted to ask this question. He said, "My father has been advised of my situation."

"Very well." Ben closed his notebook with a crack, stood up, and retrieved his attaché. He didn't offer to shake hands, and neither did Jan. "If you are innocent," Ben said with skepticism in his voice, "I trust you will be released soon."

Jan debated whether it made sense to assert his innocence, decided that nothing would be gained by doing so, and said, "Thank you, sir."

In a matter of seconds, Jan was alone in the room again. If the major had been concerned that Jan would say something inflammatory, he needn't have worried, because Ben was a poor excuse for an investigator. Jan gazed at the light fixture on the ceiling and wondered if that were where the listening devices were hidden. It didn't matter, but it gave him something to do until Fyodor came into the room.

The guard eyed Jan belligerently and rapped on the closet door with his stick.

When Jan hesitated—he was considering asking to speak to the major—Fyodor jammed him in the ribs with the stick, causing Jan to double up in pain. In spite of his discomfort, Jan began to untie his shoes. Then he removed the socks and the rest of his clothes until he was naked.

Fyodor looked amused. The guard reached into the closet and withdrew Jan's own filthy clothes and shoes and tossed them on the floor in front of him. When Jan bent to pick them up, Fyodor laid his stick against the side of Jan's head, not hard enough to daze him but with enough force to evince a groan.

When Jan had finished dressing, the guard motioned with his stick for Jan to exit the room. Jan glanced at the bed, at the clean clothes on the floor, and all hope evaporated. He felt as rigid and lifeless as a beetle suspended in amber. They walked outside into the frigid air. The cloudy sky threatened rain, or snow, and Jan perversely felt relief when he was back in the abattoir and out of the elements.

Fyodor slammed the cage door behind him, turned, and marched outside. Drewniak was sitting in the opposite corner of the cage with a bemused look on his face. Jan thought he saw relief on the faces of Petrenko and Chan. Nagy's features clearly described suspicion.

"Welcome home", Drewniak said.

November 14, 1945

Jan thought it was warmer than it had been in recent days, though the boiler kept rattling on without interruption. In between peals of thunder the previous night, he had again heard the howling of animals.

When morning came, rain pelted the metal roof, and in places water leaked into the building and splattered the floor. He felt a stabbing pain in his stomach. Had Fyodor's stick ruptured something? All he could do was squat against the side of the cage and put his arms around his knees. How he yearned for a book to take his mind off his maladies.

"Cigarette, cigar, vodka?" Drewniak inquired above the dirge-like music.

"Shut up, for God's sake", the normally sedate Lutz said. He and Schreiber had been attempting a game of mental chess, with only cement chips and bone shards from the animals that were once slaughtered here as aids.

"Let him have his fun", Schreiber said. "Anyway, it is too hard to concentrate. Where did you teach, Lutz?"

The Austrian shook his head.

"A harmless question", persisted Schreiber. "I am not asking how many men you betrayed or killed."

Lutz chewed on his lip and said, "I am a researcher at the University of Innsbruck Institute for Theoretical Physics."

David Ben seemed a distant memory to Jan. The Englishman's visit might have been eight years ago rather than eight days. The only lasting effect of the interview was the reticent, suspicious dispositions of many of the other prisoners toward Jan. He knew they suspected him of being an informer. Several days earlier, Nagy had cursed him, then apologized insincerely. Drewniak continued to converse with him, but more guardedly.

Now, curled up in response to the pain in his middle, Jan heard Petrenko's voice. "Are you ill?"

Jan didn't feel like talking. He hoped that if he ignored Petrenko, the priest would leave him alone.

Petrenko persisted, "Do you need help?"

Help? Where could help be found in this place? He didn't turn to Petrenko but shook his head.

Not for the first time, Jan told himself that death would not be unwelcome, but if he were going to die, it wouldn't be by starvation, at least not right away. Though the food was bad, he felt compelled to eat; he could not make himself leave a morsel of food in his bowl or a drop of water in his cup. Even so, the meager portions the prisoners received meant they were slowly starving; all of them were losing weight and vigor, agonizingly wasting away. Perhaps one frigid night, still half-asleep, he would crawl away from the warming pipes on the floor, shiver for a while, and let death come.

Brio said scornfully, "Help! Nowhere to be found in this abattoir nouveau."

Jan heard Petrenko mumbling in Old Slavic and knew that the priest was saying Mass, recognizing the ritual words. Most of the time, the Ukrainian was ignored by the other prisoners, but today Petrenko's concluding prayer was followed by Werner Schreiber's clear and melodious voice: "What do you hope to accomplish with all this hocus pocus?"

Jan was still clutching his knees. The pain in Jan's middle had subsided, but he was afraid to move for fear of aggravating whatever was amiss.

A blast of thunder that shook the building and the rainwater in the trenches from the leaking roof reminded Jan of another storm. Suddenly, he was back on that mountain in the Alps. On that occasion, he had been hiking along the ridgeline with two friends. Millions of leaves were on the turn, producing a colorful panorama. A storm had suddenly erupted, and the air was lit with frequent bursts of lightning. One bolt struck an old tree less than one hundred yards from where they were walking, not a good place to be in a lightning storm. That experience had been several years before the war, and Jan had been as lighthearted as one could be, considering the violent movements that plagued Europe. The trail, depressed a foot below the adjacent terrain, had become a flowing stream, prompting nervous laughter. They had known there was nothing to be done but go on, and they did, with the bravado of the young.

Jan got up slowly. He looked at Petrenko, who said, "The bad food is responsible."

"Perhaps. Or Fyodor's stick, unless you prefer to believe that I am a spy."

"I do not think so", Petrenko replied.

Jan glanced at Nagy, who was listening to the conversation with interest. "What did you do to provoke the Russians?" Jan asked the priest.

Petrenko displayed a wry smile. "It is not what I did; it is who I am that is the crime. If you are useful, you might live. If you are not ... well, look around. It was no different with the Nazis."

Jan turned his attention to Schreiber and Lutz, who were talking animatedly about their wartime miseries. "First, I lost my position at the university", Schreiber said. "After that, I was more discreet, but it did not matter. They came for me one morning and took me to Sachsenhausen. How my mistress wailed! Sachsenhausen was worse than this, if you can believe it. A cousin in the Gestapo ... he spoke for me. I was freed but warned to keep silent. After that, I hung the swastika from my window. Maybe that is the reason I am here."

"When I went outside", Lutz said, "I was always sure to have something in both hands, a trick I learned to avoid the 'Heil Hitler' salute.... How could such small-minded men have duped so many people? It is against all reason."

"They need only fool the people for a brief time", Petrenko answered his cagemate. "After they grasp power, these small-minded men, as you call them, are good at using power and keeping it."

Ignoring the Ukrainian, Lutz asked Schreiber, "Do you have a family?"

"I had a family . . . but my wife became jealous of my mistress. She took our sons to Bavaria. I have not seen them in years."

Jan glanced at Katrina and saw that she was staring at him. She seemed to be looking not at him but into him, and her gaze made him uncomfortable.

Drewniak took hold of the fence with both hands. Perhaps the Pole's action was a trigger, and perhaps it was only coincidental, but out of the corner of his eye Jan saw the young prisoner who shared a cage with the old man start scaling the fence. Up the man went, deliberately, not hurriedly, until he reached the barbed wire that framed the top. By then, everyone was watching him.

Ivan Petrenko, in a commanding voice, told the climber to come down, but he flung one leg, then another, over the barbed wire, emitting pained groans. Blood from wounds made by the barbs began to drip to the floor both inside and outside of the cage.

"Go back!" Petrenko shouted.

"Shut up", Nagy said. "Let him be."

The man descended to the floor, where he slipped in a pool of his own blood and sprawled on the concrete. Jan was surprised at the quantity of blood on the floor and on the climber, whose hands were bright red as he rose from the ground. Everyone except Drewniak had moved to the corners of their cages closest to where the climber stood.

Nagy's "Move, you fool!" was echoed in Brio's imploring and almost inaudible "*Depechez-vous, mon pauvre.*"

That seemed to be all that the climber needed. He ran for the entrance door and was gone.

All the while, the old man, the climber's cagemate, stood silent and unmoving, as far from his cagemate's point of exit as was possible.

Jan expected to hear shouts or gunshots immediately after the climber left the building, but all was quiet. Some of the prisoners resumed their normal routines, but many stood in place expectantly, as did Jan.

It wasn't long before three figures burst into the building. They were all soaking wet, and one of them, the escaped prisoner, was bloody. He was standing between two Russian soldiers Jan had not seen before, and his hands were tied behind his back. Though bedraggled and sorely wounded, the climber didn't look any more distressed than he had when he made his dash for freedom.

For the first time, Jan studied the man. In his twenties, the climber was fair haired, with features that seemed more accustomed to expressing curiosity and delight than the wretchedness he had displayed in this place. Standing between the Russian soldiers, he looked more like a boy than a man.

Without ceremony, the soldiers stood him against the wall. One of them, a tall beefy man with large ears and a great fur hat, used a length of rope to attach the bindings they had used for the man's hands to a water pipe. It wasn't necessary, because the prisoner remained docile. If he hadn't been before, Jan was now convinced that this was the outcome the climber had been seeking.

When the young man was secured, he shivered and tightly shut his eyes and mouth like a little boy resisting his medicine.

"Please, not this!" Petrenko shouted. "I beg you!"

The big Russian whipped his pistol from its holster and shot the climber in the side of the head; the loud bang reverberated inside the cavernous building.

The prisoner descended to the floor until the rope stopped him with a jerk, like a man hung from a gallows. Blood was splattered on the wall and on the Russian executioner, who wiped his face with a dirty handkerchief.

One of the soldiers laughed and shared a cigarette with his companion. They ignored the other prisoners and ignored the body when they left the building, leaving it suspended by the rope.

Brio recited:

> They have given the corpses of your servants as food to
>   the birds of the sky,
> The flesh of your faithful ones to the beasts of the earth.

They have poured out their blood like water.

There is no one to bury them.

Drewniak said to Jan, "Poor Brio, casting his pearls before swine again."

Jan tried to put this distressing event out of his mind, but he couldn't resist looking at the bloody corpse, as if he owed homage to a fallen comrade, though he had never spoken a word to this man and knew nothing about him. Brandt had insisted the dead prisoner spoke English, but in Jan's hearing the young man had never said a word in any language.

"Well, that is that", said Drewniak, turning away from the dead man. "More food for the rest of us."

Schreiber laughed out loud and said, "Not so good a menu as Sachsenhausen, where they seasoned the stew with men's bones."

As inured as Jan was to outrage, he shivered at Schreiber's words.

An open sore was festering on Jan's forearm where it had rubbed against a protruding cage wire. He could only imagine what the climber had experienced going over the barbed wire. Without thinking, he scratched it, and white pus emerged. To his horror, he noticed that something was moving in the ooze: a tiny wormlike creature. He sought the cleanest corner of his shirt and squeezed the wound until he had removed as much pus as he could, then rubbed the infected area until it bled.

"What is it?" Drewniak asked, seeing Jan's distress. "Infection?"

"Yes."

"Too bad."

Music began blaring from the loudspeakers. "A Prokofiev piano concerto", Lutz announced.

Jan couldn't find any more worms, but that didn't reassure him. He had taken a biology class at university and was well aware of scourges that aren't visible.

Drewniak said, "Ask the jailer for some alcohol."

"It is useless", Jan observed.

"I will ask", Drewniak said, "politely . . ."

Chan had finished his regimen and was sitting in the center of the cage. Nagy had his hands over his ears against the loud music. The rats kept to the corners when the prisoners were active, but Jan saw a large one near an empty cage adjacent to the boiler.

He didn't notice Fyodor and Evgeny until they were at the door of Katrina's cage. There was a rattling, the alarm sounded, then the two guards stepped inside.

Drewniak whispered, "Trouble for pretty Katrina."

Another execution? Jan could barely imagine a woman being murdered as the climber had been. He wanted to call out but was terrified of antagonizing the guards.

Evgeny, shorter than Katrina, grabbed her by the wrist. She struggled, but with little enthusiasm. They didn't bother to bind or manacle her. Evgeny kept hold of her wrist as they herded her out of the building.

"Brio, my man," Schreiber said nervously, "let us hear that verse about bird food and blood like water again."

At that moment, Jan could have throttled the German, but all he could do was growl a curse at Schreiber.

Brio said, "Perhaps I can do better ... something original:

> A malignant spirit is cast in these girders,
> Cured in these blocks.
> This building must be an abattoir.
> Slaughter is the necessary thing.
> Meatpackers slaughter.
> The Russians slaughter.
> We slaughter ... the vermin that inhabit our cages,
>   and our bodies.

"Here now! There is a poem in this if I work at it."

November 15, 1945

The Pole sat next to Jan and said, "This is a hell of a way for socialists to treat one of their own."

In spite of everything, Jan could not help smiling at Drewniak's observation.

"If you are telling me the truth," Drewniak said, "you were neither a socialist nor a Nazi, so why are you here? Perhaps you have dangerous friends or relations. Maybe Jan Skala is a bargaining chip, as the saying goes."

"If that is true, I cannot imagine the reason." Jan had no intention of saying anything to Drewniak about Frank.

Drewniak shook his head vigorously. "You are not that naïve. Your uncle is a cardinal. The Soviets despise the Church."

"It is not my Church, as I have told the major and everyone else who asks."

"Still, perhaps you are here to pressure your uncle."

"If so, they are wasting their time. He would not compromise himself for my sake."

"One never knows", Drewniak said. "The Church is political. Perhaps your uncle has information dangerous to the Soviets. You agree it is possible?"

"I suppose, but I have no knowledge of anything that would interest the Soviets." Jan didn't know Frank's whereabouts, nor had the major asked this question.

"The Russians do not believe you."

"So it seems, but the major will not tell me what he wants."

"Maybe he is testing your honesty."

"Honesty be damned! There is not an iota of honesty in this place."

Jan's vehemence proved that the Pole had touched a nerve. He understood very well that the major had tested his honesty, repeatedly, by pressuring him to admit that he had allied himself with the Germans and betrayed his country. Jan would never admit such a thing—or would he, if such an admission obtained his freedom?

In response to a sudden burst of music, Lutz announced in a distracted tone of voice, "Khachaturian again, another Kremlin darling."

"I have never heard you mention your family", Schreiber said to Lutz. "Only physics, music, and that mystic ... what was his name?"

"William James was no mystic," Lutz protested, "and I have no wife. Science—my work—is my spouse."

"You are wiser than I guessed", Schreiber remarked. "Women are nothing but trouble. Perhaps I should look up this fellow James."

Chan was manuring his plant, which was nothing more to the guards than a weed that had managed to emerge from a pavement crack. Jan envied Chan his plant and the indomitable spirit that still survived in the man.

Water from the recent rains had leaked through the roof and collected in the trenches, producing, or attracting, a swarm of gnats that didn't sting but flew into eyes and ears; one more plague, Jan observed. He examined the wound on his forearm, as he had been doing obsessively, fearful of finding another creature inside. The sore was trying to scab again, and he had to resist the urge to tear the scab away and probe the flesh.

Three figures came into the building, drawing the eyes of every conscious prisoner. Piotr and Fyodor escorted Katrina to her cage and pushed her in, none too gently, it seemed to Jan. Just seeing her again made him feel more vigorous. He tried to read her emotions, but her features and posture told him nothing.

Instead of leaving the building, the guards stood at attention near the door. Katrina wandered to a corner of her cage and sat with her head lowered. Jan thought she might be crying. Despite having awakened just a few hours earlier, and Katrina's surprise arrival, he felt exhausted and was ready to lie down and to try to sleep when another figure crossed the building threshold.

Jan couldn't say why he was so surprised to see the major, except that their jailer had given the impression of distancing himself from the uglier side of this business, the day-to-day routine in the abattoir. He wore an olive green officer's coat that extended to his calves and a traditional fur hat. Though he was bundled up as protection from the chill, there was no mistaking that waddling gait. It surprised Jan even more when the major came to his cage, opened it—triggering the alarm that Jan barely noticed anymore—and motioned for Jan to exit.

His heart began to beat so quickly that Jan thought the major must be able to hear it thumping. Was he going to be released, he wondered, or did this man have something else in mind for him? The major's expression revealed nothing.

Jan knew that everyone was watching. The major didn't say anything. He locked the cage door, took Jan's arm, and led him between the Petrenko-Lutz and Chan-Nagy cages to Katrina's, waving his hand in annoyance at the gnats. The Russian opened Katrina's cage door and motioned for her to come out, his features suggesting there was no refusing the order. Jan heard a scornful remark from Nagy, but a jerk of the major's head to identify the provocateur shut the Hungarian up.

Katrina walked out of the cage and looked quizzically at Jan, who had no answers but knew enough to keep quiet.

"Follow me", the major said, and he led them to an empty cage at the far end of the building near the big rolling door, a cage that was as isolated as could be in the abattoir. The Russian opened the door and directed them to enter.

Jan walked inside first, Katrina followed, and the major closed and locked the door. Then, without another word, the Russian shook his fur hat free of gnats and left the building, the guards accompanying him.

Jan saw that Katrina was watching him, and not the departing Russians; not anxiously, but as a cat that can take care of itself watches a dog.

"What did you do to earn *this*?" he heard Nagy shout across that cavernous space.

She said in a voice only Jan could hear, "My name is Katrina."

He adopted the same half-whispered tone, saying, "Jan Skala."

"You are Czech."

"Yes."

"I am Russian." She still exuded vitality, in spite of imprisonment and deprivation. He had been correct, he thought, in his judgment that she could not be more than twenty-five years old.

"Did they hurt you?" he said, before he had time to think about the gravity of the question.

Katrina shook her head, but not convincingly. "Why are you here?" she inquired.

"I do not know. And you?"

They sat down side by side on the floor, with their backs to the other prisoners. The gnats were less oppressive on this side of the building because there was no standing water. He thought she had decided not to answer him, and he was content to be sitting next to her, though his mind was churning with ideas and questions.

"Skala is a Russian favorite", one of the prisoners said loudly.

"Ignore them", she said. "When the Germans invaded my town, they killed my father and took me", she added matter-of-factly, as if she were relating a story from a magazine rather than an event that affected her personally. "A German colonel *adopted* me. He kept me when the Germans retreated to Berlin. In the confusion of the last days of the war, I escaped, but the Gestapo caught up with me. As a Russian, I suppose I should be grateful that they did not kill me, that they merely returned me to my colonel. As it happened, he was less of a brute than many of the Germans I met."

She paused, and Jan considered whether this pairing with Katrina, along with the meeting with Ben, was part of a strategy to drive a wedge between him and the other prisoners. There was another possibility too, an explanation that bruised his vanity.

"Why were you brought *here*?" Jan asked.

"The Soviets killed my colonel and accused me of helping the Germans. They did not shoot me for being a Nazi whore because they think I have information about the Germans. Do you think I am a—?"

"You could not have done anything other than what you did and have survived", Jan insisted. "Where did you learn to speak English?"

"My father was a language teacher. Since being here, I have sometimes wished I had never learned English. So why do you think you are here?" she asked.

That question again; if only he knew the answer. The only clue he had was the major's interest in his father and his uncle. The Russian knew about Frank, but if locating, or learning more about, him was his captor's objective, why be so obscure? There were also the major's questions about the Trotskyites, which had confused him, since Jan had never had any interest in Trotsky's brand of communism.

Jan said, "My father is a newspaper publisher. My uncle is a Catholic cardinal, but I have no idea why the Russians might be interested in them. They seem to think that I too have information they desire."

"Haven't they told you what they suspect?"

"No." Jan's answer reverberated in that open space because, at that moment, the music stopped.

She said, "They have not told me what they want from me either. Perhaps they get pleasure out of making an enemy's ... friend miserable."

Jan remembered the major's antipathy toward Heydrich's uncle. Their jailer was more than capable of acting out of sheer vindictiveness.

"Perhaps you have learned something about the Soviets they do not want revealed", she observed.

"I cannot think of anything", Jan said. "Nothing."

"Keep trying. A memory that is useful to these men might earn your freedom."

Jan wanted nothing more than to *forget* the memories he had collected in the war, suddenly recalling that unfortunate day when Frank had arrived with two junior Gestapo officers in tow: young men, spic and span, black boots gleaming. A word from Frank, and his underlings had carried off Vaclav Cermak, an assistant editor of the newspaper and a well-liked humorist and prankster. There had been no shouting, and nothing unseemly was said. When Jan had inquired after Cermak, Frank had frowned and told him to mind his own business. Jan hadn't inquired again, ameliorating his feelings of guilt by telling himself that Cermak's dark humor was to blame for the man's arrest.

"I will miss you when you are released," Katrina said ruefully, "but I will help anyone to get out of this place. Look at how that poor climbing wretch went mad and what they did to him."

"Perhaps we shall both be released", Jan said encouragingly, though he scarcely believed it.

Their evening meal was seasoned with gnats. Afterward, they sat next to each other in the center of the cage. Despite the intervening cages and the space that separated them from the other prisoners, it was obvious that almost everyone was watching Jan and Katrina as if they were actors on a stage. Katrina had been so casual, so surreptitious, that it came to him suddenly that she had curled up against him. Then she put her arm around him. Women had found him, or the status he once enjoyed, attractive, but in this hellish place, and considering how he looked, and stank, he could think of few reasons any woman would seek physical intimacy with him—desperation for intimacy of any kind and something Frank had once said to him: "The honey pot can be more effective than the clenched fist."

Katrina did not impress him as desperate for sex. Even if she was a tool of his captors, and even if he made love to her, he need not open his mind and heart to her. Still, something else held him back; regret for that night with Anicka, Frantiska's best friend. Nothing more had come of it, and neither he nor Anicka had spoken of it. He had tried to put the infidelity out of his mind, but the memory had a habit of emerging when he least expected it.

The day after his liaison with Anicka, they had picnicked together in the park by the river: Jan, Frantiska, Anicka, and three friends. Jan had felt uncomfortable, had felt ashamed, though he had berated himself for these bourgeois feelings. Anicka had done better at adopting a laissez-faire attitude. Frantiska seemed not to have suspected anything, but she was too gracious a girl to have made a scene even if she had. Frantiska's response to knowing of Jan's infidelity would have been a gradual withdrawal of affection, but that did not happen. In the end, Jan had concluded that Frantiska was too trusting to have suspected that Jan and her best friend had betrayed her.

Jan's guilt that day in the park manifested itself in suspicions of his own. Rathbon, always a puppy at Frantiska's feet, had been especially solicitous to her that day, fetching Frantiska a clutch of wildflowers, telling tall tales that made her laugh, sitting beside her during the meal on the lawn. Jan knew that Frantiska had never been attracted to Rathbon, but it galled him to see that fool fawn over her. The others surely noticed, but no one mentioned it, and Fran was courteous and friendly toward her admirer.

Katrina was stroking his arm. Jan was deeply stirred; not physically, but in a way he had never before experienced. When he whispered, "Dear lady, forgive me", he hardly recognized the words as coming from him. He was not addressing these words to Katrina, but to the surrogate for the woman he saw in his mind's eye.

He felt something like a shudder emanating from Katrina, but it might have been his imagination, so torn was he between the world of the concrete and the cage and the other world in his imagination. Katrina and Fran seemed equally real at that moment. Perhaps it was he who had shuddered.

She was still stroking his arm. "Aren't you attracted to women?" she whispered.

Did they take him for an idiot? Or for someone who had resisted giving up his secrets in spite of the deprivations he had experienced, but who would now reveal everything for sex on the floor of this dirty cage? Was the story she had told him about her wartime experiences true? He was struggling with whether to confront her with his suspicions, but what, he asked himself, would be gained? If his suspicions were correct, and if he blurted them out haphazardly, he might then be in more peril than he already was.

Katrina commenced kissing his neck and ears, almost enough to make him abandon his misgivings. He was still a man, in spite of what they had done to him! His heart was pounding rapidly, and his mind was fogging up.

Somehow, he managed to ask himself a question: Could resisting Katrina's advances be an act of penance for his betrayal of Fran?

From across the room, he heard Nagy's scornful voice, "They have sent a boy to do a man's work", and in the wake of the Hungarian's insult, laughter erupted.

"You goblin ... you Tartar ... you troll!" Katrina hollered at Nagy, but her outburst lacked sincerity. "I told myself I would not allow that pig to bother me", she said to Jan, loudly enough for others to hear. "I'm sorry", she then whispered into his ear.

The spell had been broken, and Jan was seized with indignation. Now he was smoldering, but not with lust. What did the Russians hope to gain by this shallow performance? Why would they not tell him plainly what they wanted and be done with him? The consequences be damned, he told himself, and pushed Katrina away. Her initial shocked expression was replaced with a look of contempt as she crawled to the other side of the cage. He expected to hear more from Nagy or one of the others, but there was only silence.

The black and white cat squeezed into the cage, walked over his legs, and made for Katrina. Moments later, the animal was purring. Jan shut his eyes, knowing that sleep would not come for a long time.

November 16, 1945

The sound of the rattling cage door and the alarm woke Jan. He had been imprisoned long enough to have expected the onset of consciousness to be less jarring, but awakening was always a shock.

He sat up and saw that Evgeny had stepped inside the cage. Katrina was standing next to the guard. Something about her was different from the way she had appeared the previous day—the way she now carried herself.

"I must go with him", she said to Jan in an uninterested monotone.

"I am sorry", was all Jan could think to say.

She shrugged and followed Evgeny. The guard locked the cage behind him, and both departed the building.

From the other side of the abattoir, Daniel Brio called out, "Have you lost the golden goose?"

A short time later, Piotr came into the building and transferred Jan to his former cage. When the door clanged shut, Drewniak said, "I am surprised to see you back here. What did you do to her?"

"Nothing."

"Did you insult her?"

"You saw what we saw. He did not know what to do with her!" Nagy exclaimed.

"Or maybe he knew but did not have ... what was necessary", said Schreiber, who was staring through the fences at Jan and Drewniak. "They should have come for me. I have what is necessary."

Petrenko, joining Lutz at the fence, asked, "How is the poor girl?"

Jan was tempted to respond but held his tongue.

"Poor girl? Are you blind?" Schreiber said to the priest.

"I am not blind, but I still say poor girl", Petrenko replied to the German.

"Skala," said Nagy, "you will regret last night when you are breathing your last. Or perhaps Skala and the woman are ... working together. Yes, that must be the reason for his strange behavior."

Jan had thought some of the men might draw this conclusion and was relieved when Drewniak said, "Why don't you shut up, you miserable lout?"

"I am just saying what all of us are thinking", Nagy replied.

"What *you* are thinking", Drewniak said.

"What *you* are thinking too, Polish pig."

To Jan, Drewniak said, "That insolent little Tartar ought to have his neck broken."

"I am Magyar, not Tartar!" Nagy barked, then added, "Let the Bohemian defend himself. Mind your own damned business."

"When they shoot you—and they *will* shoot you—we will celebrate", Drewniak said.

This trading of insults was interrupted by Fyodor and Piotr, who entered the building with the morning meal: old bread with tepid and tasteless broth. Jan ate greedily, though there were maggots in the bread. He had stopped examining the food, knowing that he would starve if he did not eat, and knowing that if he scrutinized the food he would find reasons not to.

"Lovely brown bread today", Lutz said sarcastically.

"Eat, man", Drewniak said in the direction of Otto Bache, who was looking more and more like an overripe plum, with big folds in his exposed flesh. The German rarely moved except to use the chamber pot, and he now slept most of the time.

Drewniak repeated himself before Bache lifted his head. The German's bald dome glistened with sweat despite the cold air and his inactivity.

"It is not worth the effort", Bache moaned.

"Better than starving", Drewniak argued.

"So you say."

"It will keep you alive. Perhaps you will be released."

"Ach. Eat my portion", Bache said to his cagemate, Brio. Then the German emitted a gurgling laugh and added, "Eat, or it will spoil."

Petrenko said to Bache, "Things might change for the better. The Americans are said to be close."

"They are on the southwest side of Berlin, according to someone who ought to know," said Bache in a rasping voice, "but let me tell you—listen to me—the Americans are no match for these Russians. . . . No, I will die here. The Russians know that my factories supplied the German army, but I was not a Nazi; I was a patriot. What else could I have done, I ask you?"

That word again: *patriot.* Coming from Bache, it had no luster for Jan. Did this arms manufacturer really believe himself to be merely a patriot?

"Make good use of the days left to you", Petrenko said to the German. "Hear me."

Bache snorted and said, "Do not waste your breath. All paths lead to darkness sooner or later. Even if the Russians release me, I could not survive in this wasteland ... streets filled with rubble, buildings ripped apart. Germany will not recover from this in a hundred years."

"You speak as if you had nothing to do with it", said Drewniak.

"Why bother with him? He refuses to admit his cooperation with the Nazis", Jan said.

"The same has been said about you", Petrenko said to Jan.

"Lies!" Jan erupted, before calming himself. In his dealings with Frank, Jan had not grown rich as Bache had; he had done only what he had to do to stay alive. Yes, and to keep others alive. There was no comparison, Jan told himself, but his rationalizing was becoming harder to sustain; at least Bache had the excuse that Germany was his homeland.

Petrenko said, "This place is built on lies. My Master was murdered by Roman *collaborators.* He forgave them ... loved them. Can I do any less?"

"Your Master is a fairy tale", said Lutz.

"It is *avant garde* to say this", said Petrenko to his cagemate.

87

"How can you believe in a merciful God with all you have seen?" Lutz asked. "In this place", he added, waving an arm.

Brio's bell-like voice answered:

You see him as a saint. I am far less awed;
In fact, I see right through him. He is a fraud.

The verse was familiar to Jan, but he couldn't place it, or the poet.

"How did a Frenchman find his way to Berlin?" Jan asked Brio.

"This woman and that woman", Brio answered him. "One of them turned out to be a bad spirit, another Apate, working for the Nazis. Poets are not known for their good sense. I was carted off to Berlin by the Gestapo, then *rescued* by these Soviets."

"I have never heard of you, or your poetry", Nagy said derisively to Brio.

"I admit ... my verse is known only by a few. Before the war, I taught English schoolboys living in Paris."

"May we hear something original?" Lutz asked.

Brio's caterpillar brows crawled until they met on the bridge of his nose. "Some other time, perhaps. I have never translated my verse into English. The effort might be beyond me ... in this place."

Out of the corner of his eye, Jan saw that the old man who had shared a cage with the climber had taken off his boots. He was holding one in his hand and standing on the cold concrete in his bare feet. No, he wasn't standing, he was moving incrementally toward the corner of his cage, where a rat was nibbling on a piece of bread the prisoner must have left there as bait. The other prisoners stopped talking and watched the man creep toward the rodent. Several feet away from the creature, the man slowly raised his hand and cast the boot at the rat, stunning it with a direct hit. Then, with surprising swiftness, the old man pounced on the rat, grabbed its tail, and slammed its head on the concrete four times in succession. As if he had just found a coin on the ground, the man thrust the rodent into his trouser pocket and sat against the fence.

"No worse than our normal fare", Nagy said loudly.

Jan didn't think he was ready to eat uncooked rat, but the idea no longer disgusted him. What was that smell? Something was surely burning.

"I smell it too", Drewniak said, recognizing Jan's consternation.

"Perhaps the soldiers are burning German carcasses", Nagy said, leering at Bache.

"This odor is not burning flesh", Drewniak countered. "I know that smell well enough."

The strong smell of smoke terrified Jan, realizing he was trapped inside a cage.

"More psychological warfare", Schreiber suggested nervously.

"They will not burn the building", said Lutz, but without conviction.

Then loud music began again.

"Khrennikov," said Lutz, "but I cannot name the piece. Oh, if I had my cello, I would make some real music!"

"I was told at Sachsenhausen that the Germans let the prisoners play music at Theresienstadt", said Schreiber, coughing and covering his mouth with his hand. "Imagine that! Do you think the Soviets would give us a piano if we promised to play the approved music?"

Theresienstadt. Jan had heard rumors about a Nazi prison camp in Terezin, but he had never pursued the truth. He sat down, suddenly feeling exhausted, despondent. Petrenko was an idiot to talk to Bache about finding any meaning in this awful place. Every waking hour was excruciating—physically and emotionally. All of their clocks were running down, some faster than others, with no one to wind them up again.

Tartuffe: That was it. That was the source of the lines Brio had quoted earlier: *He is a fraud*. At least Jan's memory had not utterly failed him. He thought of Katrina and her advances. Had he been a fool to resist her, as the others had suggested? Perhaps, as the major could not have been pleased to hear her report of his behavior.

All of the men were now recumbent in one position or another. Drewniak sat beside Jan and, as if reading his mind again, asked, "What did she say to you?"

89

"She told me she was violated by the Germans and then by the Russians."

"That's all?"

"Isn't that enough? I decided I would not add to her misery." This was all Drewniak, or any of these men, needed to know.

"Now you have crushed my tender illusions about Katrina."

"Then do not question me. Keep your illusions to yourself."

"What are you hiding?" Drewniak pressed him.

Piotr entered the building, stopped in his tracks, took aim, and pulverized a rat lurking in the shadows. The old prisoner watched with a contented expression. Then Piotr walked to the boiler and turned a dial.

"Thank you for executing that rat, comrade", Drewniak said. "I will sleep better now. Is the building on fire?"

"Everything is under control", Piotr answered the Pole as he approached his cage. "We would not want our *guests* to be harmed." Then, nodding to both Drewniak and Jan, he added, "You two might soon have wine and freshly baked bread."

"A good vintage, I hope", Drewniak said to the guard.

Piotr laughed and said, "Good enough for the likes of you."

November 22, 1945

Evgeny came into the building early that day. Jan was awake, but not Drewniak. Jan's feet were practically numb from the cold, and he was rubbing them listlessly in a vain effort to warm them up. He didn't think they were frostbitten yet because they still hurt. He had slept badly, even in comparison to the fitful sleep he usually experienced here, because someone had called out repeatedly in his sleep.

Evgeny walked to Jan and Drewniak's cage and rapped on the fence with his stick. The guard hadn't shaved, and his too-small coat was stained with food and missing a button. When Drewniak stirred but didn't get up, Evgeny came inside and kicked the Pole, not too hard, but hard enough to get his attention. Drewniak cursed and struggled to his feet before Evgeny had the opportunity to kick him again. It might have been a terrier attacking a wolfhound, considering their difference in size, but this terrier had teeth; the hound had none.

"Now!" Evgeny said, using the only English word Jan had ever heard him speak. The guard's features were expressionless, revealing nothing about where they were being taken.

Jan and Drewniak exited the cage in front of Evgeny, whose stick was at the ready. Remembering Piotr's mention of wine and food, all Jan could think about was the possibility that he might be warm again, even if only for a few minutes.

Jan walked through the open door and began shaking violently in the cold air. He crossed his arms and put his chin against his chest to conserve heat, while noting the irony that his feet felt like they were burning. The steely gray sky signaled winter was nigh. The temperature was only going to drop lower, Jan realized. How would he and the other prisoners keep from freezing to death? At the edge of a bomb crater was a pile of ashes and partially burned rubbish, probably the source of the anxiety-producing smoke. Jan thought he saw movement between the stockade slats in the corner of the former animal pens, but his fear of Evgeny's stick and the bitter cold prevented him from looking more closely.

Evgeny led them to the outbuilding where Jan had been interviewed by David Ben, opened the door, and escorted them in. Jan guessed what would come next, and he was right. Spread out on the bed were two sets of clothes, no doubt pilfered from some German home. Evgeny walked into the water closet and tapped on the sink with his stick. The order was clear. Drewniak washed himself first, and then Jan. Evgeny made them remove their clothes and wash themselves as thoroughly as could be accomplished with a washcloth and a bar of soap; no bath or shave this time. When these ablutions were not being done to Evgeny's liking, he gave the offender a rap on the head with his stick and acted out what he wanted done. At one such prodding, Jan almost succumbed to the urge to turn on the guard. With Drewniak's help, he could disarm their tormentor. But then what? This was the question that bedeviled every scheme he devised, because there was no way to escape from the site even if he were successful in overcoming the guard.

As soon as they had dressed, Evgeny inspected them like a fastidious schoolmaster. Then he prodded them outside and toward the major's office.

When they reached the building, Evgeny knocked on the door, which was opened by the major himself. Wearing his parade uniform, the Russian stood aside to let Jan and Drewniak enter. Evgeny didn't cross the threshold as the major dismissed him in Russian with an economy of words.

Only one of the two brass standing lamps illuminated the room, and the paneled walls seemed to absorb the meager light. The major's chest displayed a panoply of decorations, and on his hip was a holstered pistol. An olive military cap with black visor and red trim, decorated with gold brocade and a gold star, had been placed on his desk.

The reason he was dressed formally was sitting at the table, a beefy man in civilian clothes. Beneath his large nose with burst capillaries were a neatly trimmed auburn moustache and beard. There were generous portions of bread and cheese on the table, along with four carafes of red wine. On a serving table under the window was a plate of pearly white oyster shells, emptied of the meat. A large Persian cat sat erect and still as a statue in one of the chairs at the table.

The major said to the prisoners, "Let me introduce you to Comrade Maratino."

The big man stood and made a slight bow.

"This is Skala, and here is Drewniak", said the major.

With soothing words, the Russian gently lifted the cat from the chair and set it down upon his desk. Then he commanded Jan and Drewniak to sit.

"Comrade Maratino is composing an article for *L'Unitas*", the major continued.

"*L'Unitas* is a publication of the Italian Communist Party", Maratino trumpeted.

"Comrade Maratino is . . . ah . . . renowned journalist. It goes without saying that there could be no socialist publications in Italy during fascist rule, so our guest was forced to publish from Switzerland."

In other words, Jan thought to himself, this Italian had sat out the war.

A tan homburg with a small red feather in its grosgrain hatband was resting on the table at Maratino's right hand. "Maratino is a *nom de guerre*, in honor of the heroic Marat", the big man mumbled, chewing languorously on a piece of bread. The Italian poured himself a generous glass of wine and then filled the glasses of Jan and Drewniak. "Eat, drink", he said to them as he passed the food. He tapped the rim of his wineglass to theirs and said, "*Salute!*"

Jan and Drewniak both looked toward the major, who smiled indulgently. Then the prisoners tore into the food. Although he was cautioning himself to look less hungry than he felt, Jan could not restrain himself, and Drewniak was even less timid.

93

The Italian put down his glass and looked upon the prisoners with a satisfied expression. "Comrade Major has graciously agreed to help me with an article I am composing on Soviet justice."

Jan, finding it hard to think about anything but eating, looked toward Drewniak, whose face was impassive as he ate and drank. Jan lifted his glass and gulped, but warned himself that too much wine would be perilous.

Drewniak was less circumspect, reaching across the table for one of the carafes and refilling his already empty glass. The major didn't seem to notice, but Jan knew from experience that their captor was measuring every word and action.

"When your man drove me here," Maratino said to the major, "we passed a stockade. Are you keeping animals for slaughter?" Jan recalled the movement he thought he had seen in the pens.

"Are you certain you saw living creatures?" the major asked Maratino.

"Perhaps it was my imagination." Turning to Jan, Maratino asked, "Have you met Comrade Husák?"

Jan answered that he had not, but he knew that this Czech communist had been a thorn in the Nazis' side.

"Comrade Gustáv and I met before the war; an indomitable patriot, that man."

Patriot: the word could mean anything, Jan decided. Though he had never met the man, Jan had been told that Gustáv Husák was far more ambitious than the gentlemanly Edvard Beneš, president of Czechoslovakia before Hitler took over the country.

Who could have imagined the horrors his country would experience when, early in 1938, before the Germans had absorbed Czechoslovakia, Jan's father had used his influence to obtain an interview with Beneš. After preliminary comments were exchanged, Jan had asked the president, "Was the German government satisfied with Czech concessions?"

"There were no concessions", Beneš had replied. "Who suggested such a thing?"

"The German press is saying—"

"They will print whatever Goebbels tells them to print.... You must strike that comment, Skala, but I repeat, there were no concessions."

"Demanded...or accepted?"

"That is an impertinent question!" the secretary had barked. "This interview—"

The president had turned to his aide and shook his head, stopping the man in midsentence. "Listen, Skala," Beneš said, "your father is an old friend. I expected better from you. Tell your readers the German and Czech governments have reached an amicable agreement."

"Have you heard from Hitler?"

Consternation had played across the president's features before the man forced a smile and said, "We have an amicable agreement; that is enough. The last thing we need is to provoke ... incidents. Frankly, that is why I am talking to you. Your father suggested that he might help me tamp down public anger toward the Germans. Public anger will only play into the hands of our enemies, if you understand me."

"The Heil Hitler crowd needs restraining", Jan had suggested, noting the secretary's transparent anger.

"The Heil Hitler crowd is my business", Beneš had observed. "If I restrained everyone I am advised to restrain, our prisons would be overflowing. Effective politics is the art of what is possible. That you may print, Skala."

Not too many months later, even before Frank had commandeered the newspaper, Jan had realized that the avalanche, already in progress behind the scenes, had been unstoppable. The Germans were systematically taking control of the country. Beneš was forced to resign the presidency and to endure exile in England. Had President Beneš understood this during the interview, or had he been deluded into thinking that coexistence with Hitler was possible? Presidents were men too, and capable of being wrong, dangerously wrong.

"Soviet justice", Maratino said, interrupting Jan's memory. "I am here to learn. The Italian people are ready for truth. They know where fascism and capitalism lead: poverty ... injustice, and war!"

95

The major waved his hands as if he were conducting an orchestra. "As you say, comrade. Here are two men who pose a threat to socialism. Understand, they are treated well while we ... judge their cases."

"Of course", Maratino said offhandedly.

Jan looked out the window facing the abattoir; heavy snow was falling. Drewniak tore off another piece of bread and then did the same for Jan, saying to the Russian, "Thank you, Comrade Major."

The major filled all four glasses, emptying a second carafe. He removed a pack of cigarettes from his breast pocket and offered them to the others. Everyone but Jan accepted. The Russian said, "The Soviet Union holds itself to a higher standard than other nations, higher than the Geneva Convention." He gave Jan a sly look before adding, "Where else is wine served to suspected criminals?" He chuckled and sipped from his glass. Then he asked the Italian, "Where did you live in Switzerland, comrade?"

"You understand, I departed Italy with great sadness", Maratino said with a frown. "I was persuaded to go, I say with all modesty." He sighed and took a sip of wine. "I was convinced I could be more useful to the revolution ... if I left Italy."

"No doubt, no doubt", the major exclaimed, his shiny dome wreathed in smoke. Noting that his captor's holstered gun was just inches from his right hand, Jan briefly entertained the desperate idea of grabbing the pistol and taking hostages.

"My comrades insisted I reside at Villa Principe Leopoldo in Lugano, not as grand as it once was, but ... ah ... adequate. They speak Italian, of course, but it is not Italy, you understand ... a hardship.

"Most days, I walked to the Parco Civico and wrote like a ... demon." The flush in the man's cheeks matched that of his nose, which he rubbed with the back of his hand. "So hard it was, at the height of the war, to feed the spirits of my comrades. To relieve my heavy heart, I went out at night; Lugano streets are lovely after dark."

Jan was sure that Drewniak wasn't paying anything but perfunctory attention to the Italian, as he tore off another piece of bread and gulped his third glass of wine. With the food and wine, not to mention the warm room, Jan had almost forgotten his feet. A man in mufti entered the room without knocking and placed two filled carafes on the table, removing the empty ones. Maratino poured himself a fresh glass, and Drewniak said to him, "If you please, might I have that plate of cheese?"

"Lugano was a well-deserved reward for your hard work, I am sure", the major said to Maratino. Then, addressing Jan, he said, "Skala, tell Comrade Maratino how you are being treated."

He might have been an actor in one of the theater performances he used to attend in Prague, thought Jan, as without a moment's hesitation he looked Maratino in the eye and said, "I am well treated. We all are."

Drewniak cleared his throat noisily.

"Why are you here?" Maratino asked Jan.

"A misunderstanding, which I hope will soon be corrected."

"Not a few Italian fascists have said the same," Maratino commented, laughing at his remark, "but you do not seem the type."

"You cannot judge a book by its cover, or even a first chapter", the major observed. "Time is needed to learn the truth. Skala has not said everything he could say, not yet."

"Too bad", Maratino said, shaking his head. Then to Jan he added, "Be grateful. Comrade Major is more generous than my namesake. I see no guillotine in the yard ... hah!" The Italian grinned and said, "Your long hair needs a barber."

"And you," Maratino said, turning his attention to Drewniak, "what are you suspected of?"

Jan's companion was also flushed from the wine, and his words came slowly. "I, Comrade Maratino, have been swept up in a net. When the catch is sorted, I will be called a loyal socialist. Perhaps I will be given a medal."

"You are bold. I hope you are also truthful", Maratino said.

"With all due respect, Comrade Maratino," the major said jovially, "Lugano might have done for pamphlets, but it is not ideal training for exposing enemies of the revolution."

"As you say", Maratino admitted grudgingly. The Italian made two attempts to deposit his cigarette in the ashtray before succeeding.

"We had Cuban cigars in Lugano until the Americans and British occupied North Africa. Mussolini was good for one thing: he made sure the Cubans were welcome."

"We are not so fortunate here", the major said with a pout. "Without Comrade Zhukov's generosity, we would have no wine or oysters and precious little cheese."

"That will change when all of Europe is pacified. Communist Italy is coming, in spite of Vatican intrigue."

"Take care with your words, comrade", the major said. "Skala has an uncle in the Vatican."

"The *Cardenale* Skala?"

"Indeed."

"He is a vile reactuary ... reactionary", said Maratino, wagging his finger at Jan. "Perhaps you also."

"My uncle's beliefs are not mine."

Drewniak winked at Jan, who pondered whether Drewniak or Maratino would be drunker by the end of this conversation. He saw that the cigarette Drewniak had lain on the table was blackening the wood.

"*Cardenale* Skala is dangerous", Maratino offered.

"We are well aware of that," said the major, sweeping Drewniak's cigarette to the floor, "but he is outmanned and outgunned. It is only a matter of time."

"Perhaps," Maratino said, "the *Cardenale* will soon be swept away, and the Vatican will be only another commune."

"I will drink to that day", the major said, and he, Maratino, Drewniak, and even Jan—doing his best to hide his reluctance—raised their glasses.

Maratino shrugged and said, "The rest of Europe is not far behind Italy. Socialism is inevitable. The workers will rise up. But ... those meddling English—"

"The English are busy with their crumbling empire," interrupted the major, "Palestine, India. Whitehall and MI5 have their hands full with Irgun."

"Irgun?" the Italian asked.

"Palestinian Yids", the major answered contemptuously.

"Ah, yes ... those Jews."

"What is your opinion of De Gaulle?" the major asked the Italian.

As if needing fortification before answering, Maratino took a drink of wine. "There are better men to lead France, but the general is a ... popular choice. We shall see."

"There are many good communists in France", the major observed.

"Many", Maratino concurred with the Russian. "I am happy the English threw out Churchill on his fat ass." Looking at Jan and Drewniak, he continued, "How long before you know if these men are innocent or guilty?"

The major spread out his hands and frowned. "We must be thorough. They will be given every benefit of the doubt." The Russian's words were delivered as if by a judge who respected the principle of being innocent until proven guilty.

Turning toward Jan, the major said, "We have received a message from your father."

Jan knew alarm must have registered on his features, but he asked as calmly as possible, "Where is he?"

"Your father wants you to cooperate with us, as he is doing."

"May I see this letter?"

The major shook his head, saying, "I said nothing about a letter. I told you that we received a message."

"Is he well?"

"Who can answer that question but the man himself?"

Maratino, stifling a hiccup, said, "I would follow your father's advice, Skala. There is no sense being stub ... stubborn."

"What more can you tell me?" Jan asked the major.

"At the moment, nothing. Consider your father's advice."

Looking out the window at the falling snow, Maratino said, "Thank you for your hospitality, Comrade Major, but this horrid weather—I must depart for Berlin."

"Have no worry about that. My driver is excellent. But perhaps you would enjoy spending the night in one of our guestrooms", the major added mischievously. "You saw the little buildings when you arrived."

This idea apparently called for another drink. Then Maratino said, "Very kind, but no thank you, Comrade Major." The Italian picked up the homburg and slowly rose from his chair. He wobbled to the major and extended his hand, saying, "I hope you do not mind a good word in my next article for *L'Unitas*."

"Honored", the major replied. "I am merely trying to serve the revolution in my small way."

The more Jan saw of his captor, the more impressed he was with how subtly this man could convey a message that served his purpose.

Maratino, ignoring Jan and Drewniak, let himself out. They could see the big man trudging through the accumulating snow toward a convoy of vehicles parked behind the abattoir.

The major took hold of two of the empty carafes and carried them to his desk. Then he returned to the table, but he did not sit. "What did you think of him?"

Jan judged that this was a question having little to do with the Italian. As an answer was expected, he said, "Maratino's war was not your war."

"And what do you say, Drewniak?"

"A … ah … dago", Drewniak scoffed.

"I want to talk to you privately", the major said to the Pole, and Jan did not like the sound of it. The Russian went to his desk and pressed a button. There was still some wine in Jan's glass, but he did not dare drink it. What would he be willing to do at this moment if he thought it would produce his freedom? Lie, surely. But would he also be willing to grovel or to give evidence against another prisoner?

"Sir", he began, but the major, as if reading his mind, waved him off peremptorily. At that moment, Evgeny and Piotr walked into the room. Without looking at Jan, the major said in Russian, "Return this prisoner. The other one will remain."

Jan looked at Drewniak, but his companion would not meet his eyes. He was sure that Drewniak was drunk, but he was also convinced that the Pole knew what a private meeting with the major might portend, especially after Drewniak's display of indiscretion.

Evgeny waved his stick, and Jan followed the guard outside. Piotr walked behind him. Both of the Russians were wearing their winter coats and fur hats. There were already at least six inches of snow on the ground, and Jan, shivering again and hunching over, marched through it resignedly. Whether intentionally or not, Evgeny stepped on Jan's foot, causing him to yelp with pain. Even though he had not consumed much wine, he was almost emboldened enough to curse the Russian. They led him to the building where he and Drewniak had changed clothes and made him put on his own.

Back in his cage, after Evgeny and Piotr had left the building, Ivan Petrenko asked him, "Where is he?" Like birds flocking to seed, all of the prisoners except Bache and the old man moved in Jan's direction.

"The major demanded to speak to him."

Lutz said, "Are they going to kill him?"

"Who can say?" Jan responded.

"Where did they take you?" Lutz inquired.

"We were in the major's office ... with an Italian."

"Looking like this?" Lutz asked incredulously.

"They made us change our clothes."

"Did Drewniak say something ... objectionable?" Lutz asked.

"He drank too much, and, yes, he said things", said Jan.

"He drank too much?" Nagy piped in.

"The major's wine. And there was food. Stagecraft, that is the word."

"But real wine and real food", Nagy said.

Jan snorted. "The Italian was not bright, but he could tell the difference between a piece of bread and a prop."

"To be executed after wine and a good meal ... is not so bad", a forlorn Lutz observed.

"Not one of us will survive this place", said Nagy gloomily.

The Hungarian had a way of sticking himself to Jan's inner terrors, as if this deranged man's outbursts were something Jan might think without having the courage to express. But even in this place and even in his lowest moments, Jan could hardly imagine himself taking the walk Brandt had taken. He was almost certain that the reason he was here had something to do with his uncle, but what could that reason be? At every opportunity, the major introduced the subjects of Jan's father and uncle. When he thought about his uncle, Jan imagined that stern-looking man in full episcopal regalia, with his bony face, deep-set eyes, and high forehead. Jan also recalled the humor the man displayed when he visited Jan and his father, especially in the days before the war. They had grown apart; rather, Jan had grown distant from his uncle. It had been a rare birthday when Jan hadn't received a warm note from his uncle, but he hadn't responded in kind for years. What could that man have done to produce ripples that so affected his family?

And what of the major's mention of Jan's father? Almost certainly it was a ploy, and a rather clumsy one, which told Jan exactly the opposite of what the major had intended: his father was still free, or so he hoped.

December 6, 1945

The prisoners were desperately trying to stay warm by huddling against the warm water pipes when Piotr entered the building with two small figures in tow. Initially, Jan thought that these new prisoners must be midgets, but as they approached he could see that they were children, a boy and a girl.

"The enemies of the state grow younger", Drewniak murmured so that no one but Jan could hear. The Pole had been gone for three days after their meeting with the Italian, and the prisoners thought he was dead. When Drewniak returned, he was sullen, and only after Jan's repeated questions did he finally explain that he had been interrogated about his whereabouts and activities in 1944. Ironically, or so Drewniak said, he had been battling the Nazis from January to December, barely surviving on more than one occasion. He couldn't tell if the major believed him, but here he was, neither free nor dead.

Both children were blond and fair. The boy, the taller of the two, wore knickers, woolen stockings, black boots that extended to the tops of his calves, and a gray wool coat. The girl, standing next to him and holding his hand, wore a soiled woolen skirt, a hand-knit sweater, and boots similar to the boy's. She was shivering. The children jumped in fright when Piotr slammed and locked the cage door. As they remained at the door, stunned and still holding hands, the two reminded Jan of a vibrant chromolithograph of Hansel and Gretel caught by the witch, which he had seen in a book when he was a boy. Who were they, and why had the Soviets brought them here?

Brio was crouched in a corner of his cage, suffering from some malady. The only notice he took of the children was to shake his head and mutter a few inaudible words.

Lutz, several cages distant from the children, said a few words to them in English. They turned toward him, and the boy, in German, told him that they didn't speak English. Lutz then spoke to them in German, and no one censured him. Jan, listening intently, learned that the boy's name was Alex and that he was nine years old. His sister's name was Karla; she was a year younger. They had lived in Berlin, and both of their parents were dead. Not for a moment did Karla stop shivering until her brother removed his coat and put it over her shoulders. Now all he had for protection from the frigid air was his shirt. While Lutz had initiated the conversation with boldness, even bravado, he seemed to grow more apprehensive as time passed. Perhaps reconsidering his deliberate violation of the rules, he shook his head and turned his back on the children. Hadn't Drewniak told Jan that Lutz had once been beaten by a guard for speaking German?

The two sat together against the fence, not far from the chamber pot. Karla pointed at it, whispered something to her brother, and they both laughed, the only genuinely mirthful laugh Jan had heard in this place.

The boy said something to his sister as he pointed at the chamber pot, but she shook her head. Then she pinched her nose with her thumb and forefinger.

Ivan Petrenko joined Lutz at the side of his cage nearest the children and spoke to them in halting German. Whereas Lutz's conversation with them had been readily understandable, Petrenko's German was harder to follow. Alex frequently asked the priest to repeat what he said, and Petrenko apologized more than once for his "bad grammar".

The children's father had been a German officer, said Alex. The boy was almost certain that their father was dead, though his body had never been recovered. The children's mother had been killed when a bomb destroyed their home in Berlin. Karla told Petrenko how their aunt had screamed when the Soviets took them away. When she attempted to stop them, Alex said, one of the soldiers knocked the woman down with the butt of his gun.

Petrenko then asked the children if they knew that it was St. Nicholas Day. Alex replied that they had forgotten, but Jan could see by the shine in the boy's eyes that the news gladdened him; his sister clapped her hands together excitedly.

"Do you remember how St. Nicholas gave gold to the poor girls?" asked the priest.

"Yes, yes," said Karla eagerly in German, "he put it in their shoes!"

"That's right", said the priest. "He cares for all children, and he hears your prayers."

What good could such pious nonsense do these children now? Jan wondered. The priest was succeeding in distracting them, but he was giving them false hope. Then again, thought Jan, maybe false hope was better than none at all.

The presence of these children, and their treatment as common criminals—no, common criminals were usually treated better than this—incensed Jan. Alex was about the same age as he had been when he awoke one winter morning to find that his mother was gone. How could such a thing happen, he remembered asking himself, and kept asking even after he had grown up and learned that mothers and fathers often abandoned their families. The servants had said little, except in hushed tones, and his father had said nothing for days, humiliated rather than distressed by her departure, Jan later concluded. His childhood had vanished with his mother. Life had gone on, but the hole his mother's departure had made was never filled.

Jan considered the outrageous idea that the imprisonment of the children might be a tactic the major was using to terrorize the prisoners further, to provoke some to rashness. Lutz had already broken the rule against speaking a language other than English. But if this idea were correct, what was the purpose, as the Russians could have their way with the prisoners any time they wished?

"They want to know why it smells so bad here", Schreiber said. "Does it smell bad? All the time, I thought it was Brandt, but he has been gone for . . . how long has it been since they . . . took Brandt for a walk?"

Nagy was clutching the wire and staring at the children, who were chattering to each other in subdued voices. Emaciated and hunched, he leered at the children and licked his lips as if he were contemplating roasting them for dinner.

"Look at you, man!" Jan shouted to Nagy. "Are you no longer human?"

"I would look to myself if I were you", Lutz said.

"Damn you", Jan replied.

"Let him be", Drewniak said to Jan. "These children have upset him; they have upset all of us."

"I do not like how Nagy is looking at them."

"Yes, I understand", Drewniak observed matter-of-factly. "I would have killed that bastard by now if I could."

Jan was convinced that Drewniak's remark was no idle boast.

"Why would they bring children to this place?" Jan asked.

"Sedition", Lutz said sarcastically. "If you have not understood yet, Skala, we are all suspected of sedition; every single one of us; these children too, apparently. Sedition is a big … ah … house. Everyone can fit inside. As for these poor children, the man who said … let me see if I can translate, 'If God does not exist, everything is permitted', has perfectly described the brutes who would do this sort of thing."

"Do not bring God into this, Lutz", Schreiber said. "Isn't the priest bad enough?"

Lutz pointed at the children and replied, "I am merely saying that there are men who will stop at nothing to get their way. Do you deny it?"

The children lay down side by side on the floor against the warm pipes, sharing Alex' coat as a blanket, and Jan noticed the large hole in the bottom of Alex' boot.

"What do you think of this?" Drewniak asked Jan.

"It does not matter what I think," Jan said brusquely, "because we are powerless to do anything about it. And anger saps one's strength."

"You are in need of strength?"

"Who can tell", Jan whispered bitterly, "when one might have the opportunity to break a neck."

"Bold words, brother. We are here for a reason; even the children. *You* are here for a reason. These Russians fear something you might say or do, or something you have said or done."

Jan had no interest in talking to Drewniak, or anyone else, about why he was here. He saw Karla snuggle closer to her brother and felt a pang of regret. Frantiska loved children and yearned to be a mother—she had told him so—but Jan had feared that she would be calculating in choosing a husband and that he would not measure up in her eyes. Then came the Nazi occupation, and settling down to family life had been out of the question.

Jan suddenly realized that there had been no music that day, thus far at least. Perhaps their captors desired unimpeded conversation between the children and the prisoners who spoke German; but if so, why?

Karla, wearing Alex' blue coat, left her brother's side, crossed the cage, and began talking with Petrenko. Jan heard her ask the priest if the Russians were going to kill them. Such a question for a child to ask, he thought. Petrenko hesitated before saying that he didn't know. Then he told her that he was a priest and asked if she wanted him to bless her. "*Ja, bitte schön*", she answered eagerly, and she called for her brother to join her.

Lutz said, "For God's sake, if not mine, do not give them false hope."

"I am giving them a blessing, nothing more", Petrenko snapped back.

"Yes, and they will believe that—"

"Hold your tongue. I am only doing the little good that I can do."

Karla had to call Alex again to stir him, but he finally rolled over and joined his sister. The children stood at the fence with their heads bowed and hands folded while Petrenko blessed them in simple German.

Schreiber meandered toward Drewniak and Jan and whispered, "I take the broader view. There are times when these opiates for the masses have their uses, and this is such a time."

Alex thanked Petrenko, and then the two children went back to whispering to each other. Karla pointed at a bird that flew overhead and sometimes perched on a catwalk railing. Jan realized that the children were making a game of it; they laughed, hopped, and shouted, and then began singing:

> Deutschland, Deutschland über alles,
> Über alles in der Welt,
> Wenn es stets zu Schutz und Trutze
> Brüderlich zusammenhält.
> Von der Maas bis an die Memel,
> Von der Etsch bis an den Belt,
> Deutschland, Deutschland über alles,
> Über alles in der Welt!

Nagy cursed them loudly, prompting Chan to get up from the floor and approach the Hungarian so menacingly that Jan thought the Chinese was going to attack him. Nagy apparently thought so too, as he retreated to the fence and began to climb. Though the children hadn't understood what Nagy was saying, they knew his wrathful words were directed at them.

"No more", Chan said to Nagy.

Nagy started to answer, but Chan took another step and said, "*No more.*"

"You dirty little squirrel!" Drewniak shouted at the Hungarian.

As the Pole said this, Chan returned to his seated position, and Nagy cautiously descended the fence.

Not cautiously enough, however, as a wire end caught his sweater and tore it open.

"Now see what you have done!" Nagy said to Chan, and the Hungarian began to sob.

"Too bad it wasn't his throat", Drewniak said to Jan.

"The children will freeze", Schreiber said, as if Nagy were nothing more than a sideshow. "These goddamn pipes are worthless."

Jan wasn't certain if Schreiber was expecting an answer or if the man was just making an observation, but he said, "Surely they will be given blankets."

Drewniak said, "In my uncle's abattoir, they slaughtered piglets. To the Soviets, this is still an abattoir, but less valuable livestock than before."

As the children returned to the pipe and huddled together, Fyodor and Piotr entered the building. Fyodor, bareheaded and spinning his black stick high in the air, opened the children's cage, went inside, and grabbed each by an arm. They followed docilely, and Piotr slammed the door shut behind them.

"Damn you", Lutz muttered as the guards and children walked to the door, prompting Jan to say loudly in German, "Farewell . . . take courage." His eyes watered, and he wiped them with the back of his sleeve.

"No doubt our captors will soon see that these children are no threat and will set them free", Drewniak observed insincerely.

"They are German", Nagy countered. "That is enough."

"Chan, you have my permission to murder that snake", Drewniak said.

Nagy's eyes lurched to Chan, but the man's eyes were closed, and he did not move.

"This is the devil's work", Ivan Petrenko said in a clear, commanding voice.

"Blame it on the devil if it gives you comfort", said Schreiber. "I blame it on human nature."

"Inhuman nature," Lutz said, "but I do not need devils to explain that."

"Evil is a—", began Petrenko.

"Evil?" Schreiber cut him off. "The forces of nature . . . evolution, the survival of the fittest, psychological disorders . . . are enough to explain human choices."

"You have experienced Nazi, and now Soviet, torture and murder, and you deny the existence of evil?"

Nagy, holding the torn cashmere together with a thumb and forefinger, said, "Let's not start this again, for God's sake."

"I cannot believe I am saying this, but I agree with the Tartar", Drewniak remarked.

Could the flight of Jan's mother, the brutalization of thousands of children such as Alex and Karla, and even his own imprisonment have a scientific, an evolutionary, explanation? Jan asked himself. Was there no such thing as free will? He rebelled against such an idea, but why? Even in the story of Hansel and Gretel, the stepmother and the witch could be defended as doing what was necessary for survival in a time of famine. Yet for centuries, the witch was considered to be evil. Only in the last century would anyone suggest otherwise.

And what of Jan himself? Since his imprisonment, no, even before that, he had been justifying his collaboration with the Nazis as necessary for his survival, but couldn't his cooperation with Frank be likened to helping the witch prepare her fire?

When Fyodor and Evgeny came with the food, there was none for Jan, Lutz, and Petrenko: the three who had spoken to the children. His stomach aching, Jan could hardly stand watching Drewniak consume his meal. For a moment, Jan thought that Drewniak might share some of his food, but it was gone in a matter of seconds.

As Fyodor set down Brio's food, the sick man made no move to eat it. Fyodor poked Brio with his stick, but still the man would not go near the bowl.

"If he doesn't want that food, give it to me", Jan pleaded.

The guard smiled at him, then flipped over the bowl with his stick. If Jan could have gotten into Brio's cage, he would have licked the gruel from the floor.

Martial music began and reverberated from wall to wall, floor to ceiling. Lutz yelled, "Rachmaninoff is Russian! Why not his music instead of these grim marches?" Then he added to no one in particular, "Alas, he fled to America. He too is a traitor to the revolution, I suppose."

In spite of Jan's hunger pains, Lutz's words stirred him. He remembered being held by his mother while listening to music on their gramophone. Much later, Jan's father mentioned that she had been passionate about Rachmaninoff and the romantic composers. It was then that Jan had begun listening to Rachmaninoff recordings and was startled to realize that the Russian's music, its anguish mixed with joy, affected him immediately, and viscerally, almost as if he were back in the conservatory with his mother.

Where had she gone, and where was she now? he wondered.

Jan curled up in a ball beside the water pipe and began to cry, stifling the sobs so that the others wouldn't notice. There was no hope, he admitted, not for himself, not for those children, not for any of them.

December 12, 1945

"The swine are slaughtered, but the pens are not filled again", observed Brio. "Soon, this abattoir will be ... *fini*." Brio had somewhat recovered from several days of severe illness, but he was unsteady on his feet, and the skin on his face was stretched and yellow.

"Why do you say this?" asked Drewniak.

"We are here, together, for some reason. If not, other prisoners would be arriving. Are not the streets full of suspicious characters?"

"But we do not know each other; we are not members of the same party."

"Most of us speak English ... and other languages. We are ... ah ... characters in a play that the Russians are directing."

"You are making a sand castle out of a grain of sand."

"Perhaps. I am known for this."

Drewniak shrugged and turned his back on the Frenchman. He noticed Jan had been listening to the two of them and turned away from him too.

The rattling of a cage door followed by the sounding of an alarm diverted Jan's attention from the Pole. Fyodor was going from cage to cage, rapping on the door and depositing a piece of paper inside. When he came to Jan and Drewniak's cage, the Pole didn't turn around.

Jan picked up the paper and read it. The contents were in the form of an advisory, stating that the Soviet army had occupied most of France, Holland, and northern Italy. Before Jan had finished reading, Brio had crumpled the paper and pushed it through an opening in the fence.

"It is a lie", Brio said loudly.

"How do you know?" Lutz asked him.

"De Gaulle would never permit it."

"Even before I was arrested, the Red Army was swarming west like a cloud of locusts. What could De Gaulle do about that?"

"The Americans ... they would stop the Russians", Brio said, but feebly.

"The Americans are tired of fighting," Lutz said, "and Europe is not their home. As for the Russians, what are another million dead to them? Fewer mouths to feed."

"Do *you* believe the Russians have invaded France?" Brio asked Lutz.

"I do not disbelieve it."

Brio made his hands into fists and shook them.

"See here, Brio," Schreiber interjected, "like the Egyptians, we have been swallowed up in a red sea. Anyway, your first allegiance is not to France."

Brio glared at him and said, "You know nothing about it."

In the days before the war, Jan would have questioned Schreiber in order to uncover what was behind his reference to the Egyptians and Brio's defensive response, but the abattoir had sapped his inquisitive spirit. Noticing Drewniak's indifference to the conversation, Jan asked him, "Are you ill?"

"No worse."

"What is troubling you?"

"Everything. I have been thinking about the children. It is bad to be orphaned by war, but to fall into the hands of your enemies.... And your fate is the same as those children, eh, Skala?"

"What are you saying?" Jan demanded. "The only thing I have in common with those children is that I am a prisoner of the Russians."

"Don't be angry. I am only saying that, like those children, you have no one to help you. Your father cannot help you any more than theirs can. I am in the same boat as you. We must take care of ourselves, Skala, if we can."

"How can one look after himself when he is *en route?*" asked Brio.

"What are you talking about?" Drewniak replied.

"Do you not see?" Brio proclaimed, perking up. "This abattoir is a *diligence. Le conducteur* is our friend the major. The guards with their sticks and whips, the *laquais.*"

"And where is the coach going?" Lutz asked.

"That is obvious: to *enfer* ... no?" Brio said in a theatrical voice.

Still bearing the weight of Drewniak's insinuations, Jan did not have the energy to follow Brio. He slumped to the floor, leaning his head against the cage. The previous day, he had counted the openings in the fence that composed his cage: 5,407 openings. He had had to start over when he was in the six hundreds because he had dozed off and lost his place. Sometimes, he sat in front of an anthill that had emerged from a crack in the floor and watched these creatures' commerce: anything to consume the long minutes and hours. Looking up, he noticed a pair of doves perched on the catwalk railing overhead. Birds had been coming in and out of the building through holes in the damaged walls, seeking shelter from the weather. The birds suddenly took flight as Fyodor and two strange guards carrying rifles burst into the building.

Jan began to tremble. When the guards rattled the Brio-Bache cage door, even Bache was stirred to attention.

Fyodor, a big grin on his face, stepped inside, while one of the other guards waited, and motioned at Brio with his stick.

"Where are we going?" Brio asked, his voice cracking.

Fyodor shook his head.

"Are you going to kill me?"

Bache struggled to his feet, using the fence for support, as Fyodor banged his stick against the fence and pointed at the cage door.

Brio nodded at the guard and then surveyed his fellow prisoners. For a moment, Brio looked directly into Jan's eyes, and the Frenchman seemed to Jan more composed than he could ever have been under such duress. Then Brio threw his shoulders back and seemed to grow taller. With a grim smile, he said:

Children, I take my leave,
Much ... ah ... vexed in spirit.
I offer good advice, but you won't hear it.
You all break in, chatter on and on.
It is like a madhouse with the keeper gone.

Jan could well imagine Brio addressing his English students with this verse in headier times. Brio exhaled, shrank, and walked past Fyodor. The three guards accompanied him out of the building.

"So ends Brio", Lutz said despondently.

"We do not know that", Jan protested.

Schreiber said, "*You all break in, chatter on and on.* Brio knew."

"None of us knows anything", said Drewniak. "I thought I was finished some days ago, but here I am—"

The sound of gunfire interrupted him.

"That is that", Bache said, and his knees buckled, causing him to stumble to the concrete floor.

Jan was ashamed at the feeling of relief he had experienced when he realized that the guards had come for Brio, not him, but how many more such visits could he survive? Only nine prisoners remained. Surely, he told himself, they would take the two remaining Germans and the priest before they took him, and probably the louche Nagy. Remembering Brio marching out the door, he cringed at these cowardly calculations.

"You are wondering when your turn will come", a voice said, and Jan trembled before realizing that it was only Petrenko.

"How do you know that?" Jan asked.

"Because we all wonder this."

"Even you?"

"Certainly. I do not want to be killed."

"You are afraid?"

"Of course." Petrenko lowered his head and backed away from the fence.

All the prisoners retreated into bunkers of gloomy silence. Brandt had been universally detested, and the climber had provoked the

Russians by trying to escape, but Brio was liked and respected by most of the prisoners and had done nothing belligerent in Jan's estimation. Considering what the major knew about Jan's wartime activities, he ought to have been in more peril than Brio, an unwelcome and terrifying thought.

"Are you married?" Petrenko asked Jan, as if by conversation he could dispel the fear Jan's expression must have revealed.

"No, but I intend to marry", Jan answered curtly.

"What is her name?"

"Fran." He had told the priest he intended to marry, but would he ever see her again?

"Did you help the Germans? Is that why you are here?"

"I told you that I did what was necessary to survive, like a million other Czechs."

"If you are being truthful with me—"

"Damn you!" Jan erupted.

"Calm yourself. I am asking these questions for a reason", Petrenko said. "If you are being truthful with me, then the reason you are here might be . . . personal. Victims of . . . um . . . I think the word is *vendettas*, are often surprised to learn it. Have you read *The Count of Monte Cristo?*"

Jan remembered reading the story in the original French and how the experience reinforced his love for languages. "When I was a boy, yes, but you are speaking nonsense." Even as he said this, Jan realized that he had never considered this explanation for his imprisonment. He knew of no one who hated him, but couldn't a stranger, convinced that Jan had collaborated with the Germans, have accused him of something? How had Petrenko reasoned to this conclusion when Jan had not even considered it?

"Shut up and leave him alone", Drewniak interjected. "We are beaten men. Nothing matters."

"The truth matters. Ukraine, where I was born, where I lived, and where I hoped to die, has been trampled by the Russians, the Bolsheviks, the Nazis, and now by these Soviets. The only response to lies and hatred is truth . . . and mercy."

Nagy laughed loudly. Then he tried to say something but couldn't stop laughing.

"It is impossible for truth, or mercy, to survive in hell", Jan said, waving a hand disdainfully at their surroundings.

"Yet you say you want to marry", Petrenko said. "You desire to be free again, to live in freedom. Freedom and truth are ... married to each other. There is no freedom without truth."

"What rubbish!" Schreiber said.

"One of my comrades disagrees", Petrenko said, glancing in the German's direction.

"I am not your comrade", Schreiber retorted.

Jan said to Petrenko, "I say again, truth is meaningless in this place. You have spoken to the major. There are thousands like him in this new world."

The priest hesitated, then said, "We have talked. He is not a typical Soviet ... soldier."

"Speak plainly", Jan insisted. "Except for his rank, he is no different from Fyodor or Evgeny ... brutes, one and all."

"Quiet ... enough", Drewniak whispered. "Remember Brio, for God's sake."

"I do not listen to priests!" Schreiber snapped. "Ignore him, Skala."

"You are listening to this one", Drewniak said. "He has gotten under your skin."

Petrenko said to Jan, "There is yet cause for hope."

"There is no hope", Jan said. "Didn't you see those pitiful children, what happened to Brio? He was not a Nazi, an enemy soldier, a dealer in weapons. Brio was an artist. After Brio, it is impossible to hope."

"Impossible? I would be careful with this word. When I was a young priest in Bratkovychi, I had dinner with a man who lived on the edge of the city. He filled a small jug with sugar water and hung it from a pole ... to attract butterflies. An ant could climb to the nectar, a bee could fly to it, but it seemed impossible for any other animal to reach it.

"One night when I was leaving the house, I saw something I will never forget. A badger had climbed a small tree near the pole and was creeping along a branch. He crawled further and further along the limb, until the branch began to bend toward the jug. When the badger was close enough, he grabbed the jug with both hands, while his feet grasped the branch, and drank all the nectar. Afterward, the animal backed up the branch to the tree and climbed to the ground. Impossible, one would say."

The other prisoners had ceased paying attention when Petrenko said to Jan, "You *see* more than other men ... a gift, but do not make the mistake of thinking that because you see *more*, you see *everything*."

When the evening meal arrived, Brio's bowl was collected. That told Jan as much about Brio as the gunshots. No one dared to ask Fyodor and Piotr any questions. After he had eaten, Jan noticed that Chan was kneeling in front of his plant, which had grown to a height of almost six inches.

Chan met Jan's eyes and pointed at a little flower on the plant.

Petrenko, who had moved as close as he could to the Chan-Nagy cage, nodded his approval, then shuffled to the boiler pipe and curled up on the floor.

Petrenko impressed Jan as a dreamer, if not a fool, but how could a fool have conceived that explanation for why Jan had been arrested? Who might have hated him so much that he would try to convince the Soviets to arrest him? For the first time, Jan admitted to himself that he might have been taken for a traitor by some of his countrymen.

That evening, each of the prisoners was provided a blanket, all too thin but precious in this frigid place. Drewniak remarked to Jan, "These Russians don't want us to freeze to death ... for then Mother Nature would cheat them out of their fun."

Still chilled beneath his blanket and with his hands clutching the pipe, Jan could hear Petrenko singing a song or hymn. He could see Bache, looking like a big rag doll, lying against the pipes and was struck by that cage without Daniel Brio, whose wit had enlivened their miserable days.

It is like a madhouse with the keeper gone.

December 15, 1945

"Let us get down to business", the major said. He was sitting behind his desk and wearing his officer's coat, an overcoat, and a gray fur hat. The radiator was off, the windows were open, and Jan felt colder in this room than in his cage. He had a fever, and he had no doubt that was the other reason he was shivering.

The desktop was practically bare, no carafes of wine this time. There was a tumbler of amber liquid at the man's right hand, but the major offered nothing to Jan, who couldn't see whether the Russian was wearing his holster.

Jan had not been redressed for this meeting. Even worse, sometime in the night, the warm water pipe against which he had been sleeping had started leaking, soaking his pants with rusty water. Startled into consciousness, he first thought he had wet himself. Discovering the truth, he had crawled to an intact section of pipe, but sleep had been impossible.

"What has become of Katrina?" Jan asked the major, blurting out the question without thinking.

"You had your opportunity with the girl ... and squandered it."

"I have not seen the cat since she was removed."

"It is in the nature of cats to go off without warning."

Jan could see that his captor had no intention of illuminating him about Katrina, and he was certain that this man had orchestrated everything that had happened.

The Russian took a sip from the tumbler; then he tapped a cigarette several times on the desktop and lit it. The silence in the room was broken by a loud retort, surely a gunshot. The major paid no heed, but Jan flinched.

"This will be your last chance to tell the truth", the Russian said, giving Jan a look that said he would like to rip a response out of him.

"Tell me what you want to know", Jan implored.

The major stood, leaned across his desk, and shook his cigarette above Jan's head, dusting him with ashes. "I fear that Drewniak is a bad influence on you. I have cautioned him about it."

The major reseated himself, and Jan said, "If there is any possibility that I do not know what you think I know, then why not tell me what you suspect?"

The major took another sip and breathed deeply. Maybe he was considering what Jan suggested; maybe he was pretending. He put out the cigarette, saying, "Very well."

Jan waited. There were still several inches of liquid in the tumbler, but the major retrieved a bottle from the desk drawer and filled the glass. His eyes crawled from Jan's face to his hands, and back again, before he said, "A comrade in Prague informed us that one of Trotsky's disciples supplied you with maps and details of Soviet prison camps, that this information might have been passed to your uncle or that you might still have possession of it. The propaganda impact of these documents in European capitals would be ... unfortunate."

Jan shook his head vigorously.

"Now that I have told you, what do you have to say for yourself?"

Jan's mind was racing. If the other prisoners posed individual threats to the Soviet agenda, then Jan Skala posed a *cosmic* threat. Molotov would have been advised of such an allegation; maybe even Stalin.

"Who accused me of this?"

"Reveal everything, or I shall summon the guards, and you will be executed immediately. Say *au revoir* to Chateau d'If, Jan Skala."

Jan couldn't help but recall Petrenko's reference to *The Count of Monte Cristo*. Initially, he had rejected the notion of a personal vendetta being responsible for his arrest, and even when he had entertained the idea of an accuser, he had imagined that accuser to be a stranger. Now the buried egg of an idea was morphing into a wriggling nymph.

122

The major began to say something, but Jan interrupted him, "Give me a moment, I beg you."

In Dumas' novel, Jan remembered, Fernand's perfidy contributed to Dantes' imprisonment, allowing Fernand to marry Dantes' betrothed, Mercedes. Prior to Jan's arrest, a man he had considered to be negligible, even a clown, had managed to insert himself into Fran's circle of friends and to inveigle invitations to gatherings at which she would be present. "You better watch that fellow", one of Jan's friends had said of Rathbon, but Jan had only laughed, convinced that in everything that mattered, he was superior to this supposed rival.

"Rathbon", Jan said bitterly.

The major started. He took a drink, lit another cigarette, and snapped, "What do you mean?"

Hadn't Rathbon associated with the communists in Prague, though he had kept them at arm's length during the Nazi occupation? Perhaps someone had told him about the existence of these camps. Rathbon knew about Jan's uncle, the cardinal, a man the Soviets would fear if the prelate possessed this information. And Rathbon was infatuated with Frantiska, almost comically so.

But this was no comedy. Jan had an enemy, a man whose will and resourcefulness he had grossly underestimated. A dissimulating Rathbon had put him here. The Soviets had been only too willing to believe what they feared, and, if they made a mistake, it was only a matter of one human life.

Jan considered whether Rathbon stood a chance with Frantiska now that he was gone. He would have scoffed at such an idea a month ago, but he had never suspected how imaginative and determined Rathbon could be. Surely he would not have planned such torment for Jan without applying himself to the end game: Fran. How would he weasel himself into Frantiska's affections? Would Rathbon pose as a consoler or as an accuser feigning outrage at how shabbily Jan had treated Frantiska by vanishing without explanation?

The major's hands were folded against his lips, and he was watching Jan as if he could hear every one of these internal thoughts and questions.

"With me out of the way, Rathbon can pursue a woman he wants. It is as simple as that."

The major clearly hadn't expected this line of defense. The Russian sat back in his chair, with tumbler and cigarette in either hand. Though Jan was half-mad with rage and shivering from the bitter cold, he realized that his only hope was to press this defense as aggressively as he could.

"I tell you, this is a personal vendetta. Rathbon has lied and made a fool of you. He is the one who ought to be in a cage." Then Jan played his last card, saying, "You might as well take me out and shoot me if you expect any more from me."

"Your imprisonment is the product of one man's ... um ... treachery. This is what you claim?"

"Yes, on my life and honor."

"On your honor, you say. Hah! I have heard others deny their crimes, while we had proof that they were liars. Most prisoners will say and do anything to save their skins."

"And yet I have identified the man. I have explained why this man was eager to accuse me. You can easily check my story."

Planes droned overhead, making conversation next to impossible. When they had passed out of hearing, the major said, "No doubt they are on their way to France."

It was Jan's turn to size up his captor. He had not believed that the Russians had extended their hegemony so far, and his anger at Rathbon made him incautious. "The Americans would not permit France to be overrun a second time", he said.

The major looked into Jan's eyes with the penetrating attention of an oculist. "You do not know the Americans like I do. Don't you remember that I attended university in America?

"The second floor of the Purdue Memorial Union houses a small library and a fine classical music collection. It is not a popular place, but I enjoyed the seclusion and silence. I became friends with the docent who kept order in the room, a nice enough fellow, but soft like so many Americans. There was a winter afternoon much like this one when we listened to Mozart in that room. I returned to South

Hall very late, after curfew ..." He trailed off, and a crafty smile appeared on his froglike face.

"The Americans will not shed blood a third time for France. But back to business. Perhaps I will think about what you told me. In the end, I cannot see that it matters."

"If I have the information you desire and give it up, I must be killed as an enemy of the people. If I do not have the information, I must be killed because I am inconvenient, an embarrassment", Jan said resignedly.

"But if I conclude that you do not possess the information, your passing can be ... less unpleasant. So the question of whether you are telling the truth is not ... um ... trivial."

"I will promise not to reveal any of this", Jan said as sincerely as possible.

"I am sure your *intentions* are pure," the major said jovially, "but one cannot take things promised for things *accomplished*, especially where Nazi helpers are concerned."

"You could return me to Prague. There are Soviet troops there. If I break the promise, you can have me arrested."

"We are not all knowing. Without our noticing, you might pass along the information to a person who leaves the country. Then what good is punishment after the deed is done? It is wiser to ... detain you."

"Don't you mean that it is wiser to execute me?" The cold and fever had made Jan frenzied. He had a sudden urge to reach out, grab the glass on the desk, and drink to the dregs.

The major was watching him warily. "Why did you kill Brio?" Jan bellowed, remembering how the Frenchman had received his death sentence.

"Who said he was killed?" The major lowered his head and said, "He is back in France by now, I would assume."

"Just like that?"

"Not just like that. Our investigation was completed, and Brio was released."

Jan didn't believe the major, but he could only press so hard. He said, "Was that *wise*?"

The major's chilly gray eyes flashed, and he muttered, "We are not barbarians. Others insist I have a heart."

"So does a rat", Jan retorted.

"Hmmm ... Pushkin has something to say about this." The major paused and squinted, as if he were searching for the relevant verses on the wall. "Ah, well, I cannot translate without the words losing their ... ah ... vitality. But, Skala, Pushkin was overbold too, and it cost him his life. Europe is in turmoil. We Russians must protect ourselves."

"From what?"

"Reactionaries. Those who assisted the Nazis. Men like your uncle."

"How can my uncle harm the Soviet Union?"

"If you allow a few hornets to make a nest, you might one day discover that they have overrun the house. There was a time when the Czar believed Lenin to be nothing but a little hornet."

"You said that Brio was released, that he was innocent. Why not release me too?"

The major wagged a finger and said, "I did not say that Brio was innocent. I concluded that he is not dangerous to us. Jan Skala *is* dangerous, because even if he does not have the information we believe him to have, he now knows there is a reason for our suspicions. You see, by forcing me to reveal what we suspect, you have made your release impossible."

Jan did see the matter as the major did. And if Jan believed that Brio was dead—and he did believe it—then this was nothing more than a game of words. He was reminded of Vaclav Cermak, another man whose fate was ambiguous, whom Frank's henchmen had removed from the newspaper offices. Had Cermak been murdered by the Nazis? Liberated by the Russians? Or had Cermak's incarceration bridged German and Russian occupation, as Schreiber's had? On the day the Russian army had cattle-driven the remaining Germans out of Prague, Jan had seen Cermak's daughter on the street. Though he had desired to ask this woman about her father, shame had prevented him from approaching her.

"Would you be surprised to hear that before I released him, Brio and I discussed art . . . in this very room? He sat where you are seated. I am not a man without feeling."

What does he expect me to say? Jan asked himself.

Not waiting for Jan to answer, the major continued, "But I know that history and art are connected, Skala. Art must serve man's progress; otherwise, it is only sentiment. You know, your friend Brio had gone to seed. How like an artist who fails to understand this essential principle!"

The major emptied his glass in several gulps and rose to his feet. He was indeed wearing the pistol. If Jan was ever going to make his move, this would be the time.

"You seem to regard that shifty Yid highly. He called himself a poet, but he was nothing but a parrot. Now I have duties to attend to. Piotr will come for you shortly."

The major had taken a step toward the door when Jan said, "Where are the children?"

"What does it matter? They are German. Do you know how many Russian children the Germans killed, mutilated, violated?"

"So you repeat these crimes?"

"Such rectitude—a favorite word of one of my American professors—coming from a Nazi slave.... Children are a state's future. There will be no German future. Two German children are nothing."

The major left the room. The temptation to get up and close the windows was powerful, but Jan fought it down. A cold wind chilled him to the bone. Jan took the tumbler from the major's desk as stealthily as he could and lapped up the last few drops.

As he put down the glass, Jan heard the door open behind him. He turned around and saw that the major had reentered the office. The smirk on the Russian's face informed him that he had seen Jan's desperate act. The major closed the windows with a thud and walked past Jan to the desk, lifting the tumbler and inspecting it, as one might a test tube. Then he placed it gently on the desk and said, "I will pose a question, Skala, but first look out the window at the motorcar in front of this building."

Jan stood slowly and inched toward the window. Standing not five paces from the door of the building was a black closed-top Daimler, motor running, with two Russian soldiers inside, one at the wheel and one sitting in the rear of the vehicle. Extending from the hood of the motorcar was a petite red flag with an even smaller—from Jan's vantage point, almost invisible—hammer and sickle.

"Would you like to leave this place ... now?" the major asked him.

"You will let me go?" Jan gazed through the pane of glass at the Daimler, at the men inside, at the vapor coming from the tailpipe, at the barely perceptible vibration of the running vehicle. Then he inquired, "Why are two men inside the car?"

"Would you like to leave this place?"

Jan turned to face the major and said, "If I leave this place, will I survive the journey? These men might be more than chauffeurs."

"Take your chances in the cage or in the car. Which do you choose, Skala? Be quick about it. Perhaps the motorcar is an act of mercy."

"What do you mean by mercy ... deliverance from this place?"

"Yes, deliverance."

"I can make the choice?"

"Yes, this time."

Jan's hands were tingling, and he realized that he was panting. He was incapable of anything more than fragmentary ideas. Perhaps, he told himself, this *was* an act of mercy, or what passed for mercy in his captor's devious mind. Jan might get inside the warm Daimler, take a ride with these men, and be finished with all of this. During his time in the abattoir, which seemed like an eternity, Jan had learned that there were worse ways to die.

No, this had nothing to do with mercy, nor had the open window been a tactic to compel Jan to be more forthcoming. His captor enjoyed inflicting pain for pain's sake, enjoyed breaking men for the sake of seeing them broken. There were things Jan's captor wanted—maybe needed—to know, and he would doggedly pursue these things, but he would also prey on his captives' desperation and revel in it. To pretend otherwise was delusional, wasn't it?

The major was smoking and looking out the window when Jan walked to the door, opened it, and stepped outside. It was cold, but he could feel warmth radiating from the Daimler. Through the windscreen, he could see the two men. The pungent exhaust fumes caused him to cough, and he had to turn his head to get his breath. He walked to the passenger door and looked inside at the men, neither of whom would meet his gaze.

Jan's hand was on the door handle. All the resentment, rage, misery, and despair of the past two months rushed in and pressed Jan to open that door. Perhaps the Russians would ferry him to Berlin, give him a hot tub and some clothes, and let him go. Or perhaps they would shove him out of the car into a frozen field and put a bullet in his head. Would not either of these outcomes be better than going back to the abattoir?

The driver began tapping on the steering wheel with his finger. Jan was sure that if he turned around he would see the major's face looking at him from his office window.

Jan's hands were shaking and his legs were unsteady as he circled the vehicle and trudged back toward the abattoir.

December 16, 1945

Jan had been sleeping soundly, for how long he could not say, with the incessantly bright lights and loud music. He awoke to see Chan gripping the fence and staring at the cage opposite his own. Instead of its usual serenity, the Chinese prisoner's face wore a stricken expression.

"What's wrong?" Jan asked as he rose to his feet.

Before Chan could answer, Jan saw the old man lying on the floor of his cage in an unnatural, supine position. His eyes were open, and a wound in his neck was making a pool of dark blood under his head. His lacerated hands were also bleeding.

"What happened?" Jan asked numbly.

"Dried blood on wire", said Chan. "He climbed fence; he fell."

Drewniak had joined Jan at the fence and was gazing at the body. "Why would the old fool climb the fence?" he asked no one in particular.

"Maybe he climbed fence and used barb wire to cut neck", Chan offered.

"Suicide?" Drewniak protested.

"Why not?" Jan asked. "There are worse ways to die."

"This will mean trouble", said Lutz, who had risen and walked to the fence closest to the others. "Our captors do not like to be cheated out of their ... ah ... recreation."

Jan said, "We are not at fault, and we could not have prevented it."

"Skala," Lutz said scornfully, "you talk as if you just arrived here. Whether we could have prevented this death will not matter to the Russians."

Of course, Lutz was right, Jan admitted to himself.

No one seemed to know anything about the old bearded fellow, except that he had been an expert ratter. No one recalled hearing him speak a single word, not even to the climber when they had been cagemates.

Drewniak looked up at the roof and shouted, "There is a dead man in the building!" Then he repeated himself two more times, even more loudly.

That woke, or got the attention of, the others: Schreiber, Petrenko, Nagy, and Bache.

Jan knew that their captors had planted listening devices in the building, but to see Drewniak acknowledge this so directly was startling. As Jan waited for something to happen, it occurred to him that the first death he had witnessed here, the execution of Brandt, had provoked panic in him, even physical illness. Since that day, the climber, and probably Brio, had been killed. Though he was unsettled by the old man's suicide, Jan realized that he was growing accustomed to the deaths of his fellow prisoners, that the immediate shock was swiftly followed by mind-numbing accommodation. In this case, he had been hard pressed to summon any emotion at all.

Drewniak said, "I doubt if our captors can hear every conversation in this building, but they must have heard my announcement. Perhaps it will go better for us because we gave them the news ourselves."

Chan raised his eyebrows but did not disagree with the Pole.

When the guards arrived, they were accompanied by the major, reinforcing the seriousness of this matter. Evgeny and Fyodor entered the old man's cage and examined the body. Then Fyodor said several words in Russian, and the major nodded his head. A third guard, with a small head, massive body, and horny skin, stood outside the cage, pointing his rifle at first one prisoner and then another.

"What happened here?" the major demanded of the onlooking prisoners.

Silence. No one, Jan included, wanted to meet the major's eyes, as if doing so would put him in the scapegoat's seat.

"Who first noticed the body?" the major pressed them.

"I did", said Chan.

"You did, Charlie? What did you see, and when?"

Chan said, with more tranquility than Jan could have summoned, "When I awoke, body was just so."

"Just so?" the major said mockingly.

"Yes."

"Who drove this man to kill himself?" asked the major, scanning the faces of the prisoners.

"Perhaps it was the cuisine", Drewniak observed, causing Jan to wince.

"Shut up!" the major bellowed, scowling at Drewniak. Then he grinned and said, "A healthy, happy man does not kill himself."

Tempted to take the bait, Jan clenched his jaw, but Petrenko was less circumspect, saying, "He was driven to kill himself because he was made into an animal for slaughter."

The major advanced briskly toward the priest, and, like a puppy expecting a treat, Evgeny trailed him. "A fascinating theory, *Mr.* Petrenko," said the major, "and who are the villains who committed this crime?"

"You are following orders, so the greater guilt is with your superiors."

Shut up, Petrenko, Jan said to himself. *Shut up!*

The major squinted at Petrenko, looked down at the dead man, and sighed with mock concern. Then raising his eyes to Chan, he said, "Charlie, come with me."

Why not take Petrenko? Jan wondered. Hadn't the priest challenged the Russian? Yes, and perhaps he had done so intentionally, Jan thought, in order to deflect the major's attention away from Chan, but their jailer was not going to let Petrenko manipulate him.

The guard opened Chan's door, and the major stepped inside, but instead of confronting the Chinese, he went to the corner of the cage, bent down, and plucked the plant from the crack in the concrete. As he left the cage, he dropped the plant on the floor and ground it with his boot.

The guards led Chan out of the building but did not bother with the dead body. Good God, thought Jan, shuddering, are they going to leave the corpse for the rats?

All of the prisoners were still standing in place, everyone afraid to speak, when the building door burst open again, and the major reappeared, but without the guards. He ignored everyone as he made for the Lutz-Petrenko cage. He didn't bother to open the cage door, but it was clear that his intended object was Petrenko.

The priest, for his part, approached the major, grasping the fence.

The Russian lifted his right hand and displayed a small loaf of brown bread.

"Make this bread holy."

"You know that I cannot do this", Petrenko replied, with barely suppressed anguish.

"If you do not do as you are ordered, you will be ... disciplined. You will not like it."

"I cannot. Why would you ask it of me?"

"I do not ask; I command. Perhaps you are thinking about glory, but even if I kill you, no one will ever know. If you make this bread holy, I will release you. You have my word. These others have heard it. My honor is at stake. No one else will ever know how you bought your freedom."

"No one?"

"Your God will understand. Is it not said that he is Lord of the living? You will be allowed to live if you do as I command."

Petrenko said to the Russian, "It was wrong of you to destroy Chan's plant."

"You rebuke me, *Mr.* Petrenko? How can you expect me to allow that?"

"Not a rebuke, a summons."

The major glared at Petrenko and said loudly, "Evgeny!"

The guard came into the building and trotted to the Lutz-Petrenko cage.

"Teach *Mr.* Petrenko a lesson", the major commanded the guard.

Evgeny unlocked the cage door, walked inside, and struck Petrenko on the side of the head with his stick.

"Stop it, you bastard!" Jan shouted.

The major turned to Jan and put a finger to his lips, as if he were Jan's advocate, his protector from a similar fate.

Ivan Petrenko fell to his knees while Evgeny battered him. Lutz scuttled to the opposite corner of the cage. Petrenko twitched beneath the blows like a fish recently removed from a hook. Would the priest survive this brutal assault? Finally, the major ordered Evgeny to stop and said to the other prisoners, "Let us hope he has learned his lesson."

On his way out of the cage, Evgeny kicked the motionless Petrenko. He strolled over to Jan's cage and laid his stick against the fence to confirm that he had heard the insult, giving Jan no doubt that the guard was eager to inflict punishment on him as he had on Petrenko.

As Evgeny sauntered away, Drewniak whispered to Jan, "Tell the major what he wants to know. Maybe he will let you go before you are beaten or executed."

"It is too late for that", Jan said. "Is he dead, Lutz?" he called to the Austrian, who was standing over Petrenko.

Lutz shrugged and said, "I told you he was a fool. Now he has come to this."

Yes, a fool, Jan agreed in his mind. It would have been easy for Petrenko to have prayed over the bread. He could have made up something, for all the Russian would have known. But instead, here he was sprawled on the floor, stupefied, or worse.

"I think he is dead", Lutz said, crouching before the priest.

"He asked for it", said Drewniak.

Who hadn't *asked for it* in some way? thought Jan. Hadn't he himself called the major a rat and Evgeny a bastard, not to mention his service to Frank? If Jan was going to die here—and he *was* going to die here, he acknowledged to himself—then how did he want to die? Did he want to die on his own terms, the way the old man did? Did he want to be killed suddenly by someone else pulling a trigger? Did he want to be beaten and left to die slowly, painfully?

Jan's arms and legs were covered with sores, fed upon by tiny vermin. He was now more skeleton than man. His friends and family had probably given him up for dead. So then, how did he want to die?

As the day progressed, Petrenko shuddered and moaned, evidence that he was not yet dead, but it couldn't be said that he moved. Lutz gave the priest a wide berth, as though he were a leper.

When Fyodor and Evgeny brought the evening meal, Jan was surprised to see Chan with them. In spite of not hearing shots in the yard, Jan had assumed the prisoner had been executed.

Before they distributed the food, each of the guards grabbed the old man by one leg and dragged him out of the building as if he were a dead dog. That unlucky cage, with its crowning barbs, was empty. Was it *happy*, Jan wondered, to be rid of its inhabitants? Were these cage doors maws that admitted men and then vomited them out, or spit out the bones, when they were finished with them?

After Fyodor and Evgeny had departed, Jan approached Chan and said, "I am glad to see you."

Examining the comatose Petrenko, the Chinese asked, "What happened?"

"He was beaten. What did they want from you?" Jan asked, noticing blood oozing from Chan's left ear.

Chan, bending over the spot where the plant had been growing, did not answer.

Something snapped inside Jan. He looked up at the roof, imagining thousands of tiny receivers in the girders and panels, and shouted, "Rot in hell, Russian swine!"

"Shut up, you idiot!" Drewniak hissed, grabbing Jan by both his shoulders.

"Enough, Skala", Schreiber said, but gently. "You will only bring plague on all our houses."

Jan had opened his mouth to shout another insult when he saw that Ivan Petrenko had risen to his hands and knees. The Ukrainian raised a hand, almost tipped over, but steadied himself and whispered, "Be still."

Those barely audible words pacified Jan as the admonitions of the other prisoners could not, and he slumped into a corner, screwing his eyes shut.

Until his last meeting with the major, Jan had found a measure of relief from his physical and mental miseries by closing his eyes and trying to remember, in as much detail as he could summon, things he and Fran had done together: evenings at their favorite café, the food they shared, the books they enjoyed discussing, their hand-in-hand walks along the river, the ridiculous stories he told that used to make her laugh. Now even this small consolation had been taken away, because he could no longer picture Fran without seeing Rathbon next to her.

Groans interrupted Jan's thoughts. Nagy was having some kind of fit: his eyes were rolled back, and he was leaning this way and that way as though he were on a train making severe turns.

"Should we call for the guards?" Jan asked.

Drewniak laughed and said, "Even if they came, what could they do?"

Schreiber said, "Perhaps the side of a stick would do him good."

"I am certain it would do that weasel good", said Drewniak.

December 17, 1945

From the time Jan had been abducted, he had been *forced* to consider his own death. He had once hoped, even believed, that he would be released and that he might resume a normal life again. Like the sine waves he had drawn in school, the sequential peaks and troughs of hope had risen and fallen, but over time the peaks had become shorter and less frequent, while the troughs of despair had grown longer and deeper.

Jan had witnessed death often enough during the war, but he had built an emotional wall between those who were killed and himself. In public, he acknowledged the perils of the times and his own mortality, but privately he believed that he would survive.

His imprisonment, however, had extinguished that sense of indestructibility. The major had suggested that the Russians could not allow Jan to live, and Jan believed him, knowing that he posed a threat to the Soviets. His life—and the injustice of depriving him of it—was meaningless to these Russians. His execution might occur at any time, now that he and the major had reached this understanding, and he had a recurring vision of himself standing in the yard, shivering and weeping, his hands tied, with Piotr or Fyodor holding a pistol to the side of his head.

Petrenko, with the support of the fence, had been able to rise from the floor and stand. His wounds seemed to be healing, though anguish had permanently etched itself into the Ukrainian's features. Who could tell what Evgeny's stick had broken inside him? Despite the man's beating, Jan was envious of Petrenko's faith. Perhaps, he told himself, it was better to delude oneself about death, to believe death to be a passage, a gateway, a metamorphosis, than to stare into the abyss as Jan was doing.

Nagy was propped in the far corner of his cage, characteristically sullen, prompting Jan to wonder whether the Hungarian remembered his fit of the previous night. When the evening meal arrived, he grumbled, "We are given food the dogs will not eat. If this filth can be called food."

"Shut up," Schreiber warned the Hungarian in a subdued voice, "or you will end up like Brio."

"Do you think what we say makes any difference?" Lutz asked Schreiber. "They do what they want to do, and we pretend that we can influence their decisions by what we say and do. Nonsense."

Drewniak boomed, "If we are good boys, we might live until the Americans free us!"

Piotr looked over at the Pole and said, "The Americans do not care what happens to you."

Though they still spoke like men, Jan realized that the miseries of this place were making all of them into children, psychologically speaking, with outbursts and petulance replacing reason. Or perhaps, he told himself, this experience was merely revealing who they really were, the people they were able to cover up in polite society.

The big guard departed after the food had been served, but Evgeny stayed behind and personally checked each cage door. Well aware of Evgeny's hair-trigger temper, no one said a word to him, not even Drewniak. After Evgeny had left the building, Schreiber said, "It does no good to antagonize them."

"You are a coward", Nagy said to the German.

"I might be a coward, but I am not a ... lunatic", Schreiber answered, shaking his fist at Nagy and sitting down to eat. Bache crawled toward his bowl, and when he reached it, the German bent over the food as a dog might have done, sniffed it, and crawled back to the warm pipes.

"Please eat!" Petrenko shouted to Bache, his voice cracking, but the German ignored him.

"His palate is too refined for this gruel", Drewniak said between mouthfuls.

"Do not remind me of the dinners I so enjoyed before the war!" Lutz exclaimed.

"Lutz, you have never told us how you found your way from Austria to this place", Schreiber said.

"I am not obliged to tell you, but you might as well know that the Soviets are interested in nuclear fission, especially after the American bombing of Japan. So far, I have resisted cooperating with them. I did not become a physicist to make superbombs."

"Didn't the Nazis force you to cooperate?" Schreiber inquired.

Lutz grinned and said, "I gave them bad advice."

In a subdued voice, Schreiber asked, "Then why do you not do the same thing with these Russians?"

"Because the closer scientists come to producing an atomic bomb, the more difficult it is to deceive them."

During intervals when the music was less loud, Jan could hear the wind whistling. Ever since Piotr and Evgeny had entered the building, the wind had intensified, and openings in the walls and roof were acting like apertures in wind instruments, creating a doleful sound whenever the wind freshened. Looking around at this wreck of a building, Jan wouldn't have been surprised to see the metal roof peel apart.

Before long, the prisoners began curling up as close to the pipes as possible, pulling their flimsy blankets tightly about them. Jan closed his eyes. He didn't feel sleepy, but he desperately yearned for sleep as respite from the cold and his miseries. Perhaps the Americans would liberate them, he thought, his hope rising again. Not if David Ben's attitude was typical of the Western allies, he reflected, descending back into the trough. If only he, Jan, could manage to overcome a guard and get outside, could he commandeer a car or a truck and get to the road before he was apprehended? Perhaps he could talk Drewniak into assisting him in such a gambit. If he was going to die anyway, and soon, then why not do something bold?

With such thoughts, Jan's mind was too active to sleep. He sat up and looked around, recognizing that something was missing: there were no rats. In spite of the bright lights and the loud music, rats almost always emerged after the prisoners had hunkered into their warming positions, having learned that the men did not like to move once they had reclined and crowded the pipes. Jan had even come to recognize certain rats by their movements and physical characteristics. Maybe the Russians had poisoned the rats, or maybe they were gorging themselves on refuse in the yard.

Lying back down, he imagined getting inside a truck, slamming the door, turning the key, putting the vehicle into gear, and lurching toward the road, leaving shouting and shooting men in his wake. In the end, he told himself, he would almost certainly be captured or killed in the act of stealing the truck, or on the road, or in Berlin if he managed to make it that far.

He must have fallen asleep, because when he next opened his eyes the bright cage lights were extinguished; no music either. Perhaps the silence had awakened him. It was dark, but not pitch black, with gray light being emitted by scattered old abattoir lamps on the walls and by an electrical panel near the boiler.

The cold breeze was stronger than anything he had ever experienced inside this building. As comfortable as it was possible to be on the floor, Jan compelled himself to get up, not knowing why the urge to stand was so strong but sensing that he must heed it.

Most of the men seemed to be sleeping, or making a pretense of it, but Chan too was standing and looking about. Jan looked down at Drewniak and was surprised to see that his cage-mate's eyes were wide open. Then, something like a growl sounded near the main door; surely, he told himself, the sound was the wind passing through a crevice in the wall or roof.

He moved to where he could view the main door and saw that it was open. So, that was the source of the draught. Snow was blowing into the building and swirling at one of the wall lamps, and in the lamplight was a moving shadow.

Jan doubted his own eyes until a loping shape lurched toward an object directly inside the door—a burlap sack.

"Wake up!" Jan shouted as loud as he could. "An animal is inside!"

Chan crouched low as a wrestler might have done, and Drewniak, crawling to his knees, cursed and said, "A wolf!"

The wolf, followed by two others, trotted a few paces toward the sack, gripped it in his teeth, and shook it violently. The creature must have shaken something loose from the sack because the other two beasts lunged at objects on the ground.

Someone had tossed a sack of food into the abattoir, enticing the animals inside, Jan concluded. The wolf with the sack in its jaws was the biggest of the three, and after it succeeded in tearing the bag apart, it snarled at the others, keeping them at bay, until it had eaten most of the contents. Mesmerized by these darting, snapping animals, Jan, Drewniak, and Chan said nothing until the lead wolf crept to Bache's cage and pushed at the door with its long snout.

The door opened, and no alarm sounded. Jan tried his cage door and found that it too was unlocked. "See to the doors", he shouted, pressing his back against his own, while the other prisoners, except for Bache who was stirring on the concrete floor, immediately heeded his advice.

Jan and the other men shouted for the guards, but no guards appeared.

Schreiber turned the air blue in both German and English before saying, "This was planned. Unlocked doors, no alarms."

It *was* planned. Jan had already reached this conclusion. The night-time baying, the movement he had seen in the stockade—wolves must have been reconnoitering the area, and the major had found a way to make use of them.

The wolf that had pushed Bache's door open crouched and snarled at the prisoner. The animal was preparing to lunge at Bache, who had struggled to his feet and was backing away toward the far side of the cage. Jan yelled, "Throw the pot!" Bache did as Jan commanded, and the empty metal pot clanged on the concrete floor in front of the wolf. The startled animal sprang backward, and Jan grabbed his food dish and used it to rattle the cage. Lutz did likewise; Chan too.

Before he had time to consider what he was doing, Jan was outside his cage, striding purposefully toward the wolf. He stopped less than six feet from the animal, which growled at him, giving Jan the impression that it was preparing to attack. The other wolves had crept forward and were now flanking their leader. Still, Jan stood his ground, shouting at the beast and brandishing his bowl, a pitiful excuse for a weapon, no better than being empty handed.

Chan joined Jan, making a screeching sound, waving his arms, and thrusting his leg menacingly. The wolf appeared confused by the wild actions of the two men and the din of rattling cages. Followed by the other two wolves, it bolted for the entrance door. Almost immediately, gunshots sounded in the yard.

Jan's heart was pounding violently as he forced himself back into his cage, not wanting to be found on the abattoir floor by the guards. Chan did the same. After he was back inside, Jan slumped in a corner, not caring that he was sitting in rusty water from the leaking pipe, and shivered uncontrollably.

Displaying no evidence of urgency, six guards entered the building. Nagy shouted at them, "Vultures! Pigs!"

One of the Russians trained his rifle on the Hungarian, causing him to cringe and moan. Seeing Nagy's distress, the soldiers laughed.

After the Russians secured all of the cage doors and left the abattoir, Schreiber said, "Before my arrest I heard that wolves were roaming the outskirts of Berlin, but these beasts wouldn't enter an armed camp."

Petrenko added, "In my country, wolves are hunting whatever can be run to ground."

Certainly, the wolves' habitat and natural prey had largely been destroyed in the war, but Jan found it impossible to believe that these animals had found their way into the abattoir on their own. Was this little drama a piece with the children and the motorcar in the yard?

"Was Bache worth it?" Drewniak asked Jan quietly, so that no one else could hear.

Jan knew that his decision to confront the wolf had not entirely been about Bache. In truth, these wolves were not so different from the person he had been, and not just from the time he was arrested by the Soviets. Ever since Frank had assumed control of the newspaper and made Jan his vassal, he had been scavenging for privileges and little luxuries, while doing his best to hide these feral urges from Fran. If these creatures were desperate, at least they were dumb beasts.

Though he hadn't made a rational decision to exit the cage, Jan had acted to rescue a part of himself buried so deep that he had doubted whether he would ever be able to retrieve it.

The lights and music came back on, making Jan flinch; back to normal. But, perhaps, not the old normal, Jan told himself, looking at the pathetic German for whom he had risked his life.

December 25–26, 1945

Jan was rowing Frantiska down a river lined on both sides with tall linden trees. The day was warm and sunny, and Jan had that vigorous feeling that often came over him in nature. The languorous river sparkled in the sunlight, and they were close enough to the riverbank for Jan to smell the lindens' fragrant blossoms. The rowlocks creaked as the oars splashed in and out of the water. Whenever Jan looked into Fran's big bright eyes, they both laughed as if they had not a care in the world.

The cold, hard awakening inside the cage was jarring, but even the frigid morning could not wholly dispel the magical dream. Jan was as warm as was possible on the concrete floor, wrapped like a mummy in the dirty blanket he treasured more than anything else he possessed. He closed his eyes again, yearning to recapture the dream.

"Another day, Skala. Who knows what joys await us?" a bearded and bleary-eyed Drewniak said. As Jan realized that falling asleep again was now impossible, he stood up, using the blanket as a scarf to keep the chill off his neck and shoulders. When he finished scratching his head, Jan saw that a clump of hair had come loose from his scalp.

Petrenko was moving in the adjacent cage. The priest had not fully recovered from Evgeny's beating, but he could stand and shuffle about.

Lutz let out an anguished moan and scuttled for the chamber pot.

A convoy of airplanes could be heard flying overhead, whether traveling east or west, Jan could not guess. If the major was to be believed, they might be supplying Soviet forces in France. The roar of their engines was soon drowned out by a blaring score.

"This must be our Christmas music!" yelled Drewniak.

Was it Christmas? Jan recalled one boyhood Christmas, after his mother had left, when he and his father had attended a Mass said by his uncle at the Prague cathedral. The church had been decorated with fragrant evergreen branches and a manger scene with life-size figures. After Mass, Jan and his father had eaten at his father's club, a place Jan was rarely invited to visit and where the table linen was stiff and dazzlingly white. His father had even allowed him to sip wine from the boy's own wineglass.

Jan's memory of that Christmas long ago was interrupted by Petrenko, who said loudly, "I want to say something to you." The priest was standing at the fence facing the Chan-Nagy cage, but it was clear that he was addressing all of them. His features were pinched, and he had to grip the fence tightly to stay erect.

"No Christmas sermon", Schreiber retorted. "Isn't this music bad enough?"

"No sermon, my friend. I have something else to say." Petrenko took a deep breath as if he were trying to summon enough strength to speak above the music. "I have often pretended to be a humble man, but I ate and drank well. My ... ah ... parish, poor as it was, paid for these ... luxuries."

"Why eat like a dog when you can have better?" interrupted Drewniak, and Nagy barked with glee.

"So it seemed to me, but I was never at peace with myself."

"Why are you telling us this?" asked Schreiber.

"Until lately, I had told myself that this was a small matter. I have never confessed it, and now I do not think I will be able to confess again."

"We do not want to hear your confession", Schreiber said. "Kindly keep your sins to yourself."

"You cannot forgive me, but I still must confess. Yes, I am admitting that what I did was wrong."

Schreiber said, "Wake up, man. This is nothing compared to the wrongs done to us."

"Schreiber is right", said Nagy. "See what they are doing to us? They are poisoning us." The Hungarian pointed a finger at Lutz, who for the past two days had been afflicted with dysentery.

No one responded to Nagy. In fact, many turned their backs to him. "Listen to me!" he shouted. "My father poisoned my mama. It's no lie! And when I took him to task, he beat me. See the bruise ... right here!"

The Hungarian fell to his knees and began weeping. "My father was a good Christian", he moaned.

"A boy should not be beaten by his father", Petrenko said gently to him.

"How else is he to learn?" Nagy snarled. Then he wiped both eyes with his sleeve and said, "You try to make me eat, but I am no fool. They will not poison me the way he poisoned my mama, and Lutz; that fat German too."

Bache was no longer fat, Jan observed, and it would not surprise him if the German were soon dead. The episode with the wolves seemed to have sapped what little strength Bache had left.

When the horny-skinned guard came into the abattoir with old Heydrich, Schreiber said, pointing at Lutz, "This one is sick. He was awake all night. He needs something."

"We will call a doctor right away", said the Russian, laughing. Then the guard walked to the side of the cage where Lutz was reclining and stabbed the man through the fence with his stick.

"Poisoners!" Nagy shouted at the guard as he exited the building.

Drewniak said, "I miss Brio's poetry. Nagy is a poor entertainer, though his comedy has its moments."

Jan would have liked to believe that Brio was back in France, making a new life for himself, but he couldn't imagine the major freeing him, or any of them. "Brio was a *maquisard*, wasn't he?" Jan asked.

"Brio was a Zionist. I suspect that was his undoing", said Schreiber. Having gotten the attention of Drewniak and Chan too, Schreiber added, "You did not know Brio. Listen, I met the man in Paris before the war. His real name was Daniel Brionsky. Brio had genuine affection for France, yes, but his passion was a Jewish state in Palestine. Need I remind you that the Soviets are suspicious of Zionism?

"Brio was more than a poet, a teacher. It was well known that he was a leader in the movement. This must be why Brio was brought here, and why he was killed. If he had kept to poetry, he might still be alive, but if I had kept to economics, I might have missed out on Sachsenhausen and this ... ah ... delightful place."

Jan had no response to Schreiber's assertion about Brio. The German continued, "Brio once said in my presence that he feared he would become another Dreyfus. You remember that wrongly accused French Jew. Brio has—had—a daughter named Ofelia. She would be about ten, if she survived the war. The girl's mother was killed fighting Franco in Spain."

"How did Brio find his way to Berlin?" Jan asked.

"Don't you remember that Brio said a woman was responsible?" Schreiber answered him. "He must have been targeted by the Russians. Who can say where and how he was arrested. Chaos is the ally of villains, and all Europe is in chaos."

Another loud and ponderous musical score had just commenced when Piotr entered the building and walked toward the cages. The large man was bearlike in his winter coat and fur hat. With his stick in one hand and a broom in the other, he lumbered past Bache's cage, stopped in front of the door of the Petrenko-Lutz cage, and raised his stick, pointing it at the priest.

"Haven't you had sport enough with him?" Jan roared.

"Quiet. You will have your turn, I promise you!" Piotr snapped.

None of the other prisoners said a word, their eyes trained on the ground at their feet. Even Nagy had been pacified by the menacing guard.

"I keep my promises, little dog!" Piotr yelled at Jan as Petrenko shuffled out of the cage. The guard led Petrenko to the tallow area and handed him the broom, saying something Jan couldn't hear. The Ukrainian, despite his frailty, lost no time in going to work on the floor.

As Petrenko swept, Piotr often slapped him between the shoulder blades with his stick, but the priest and the guard were conversing too, which seemed odd to Jan, who expected Piotr at any moment to rear back and lay waste to Petrenko with his stick. Finally, Piotr knocked the broom out of the priest's hands and prodded him back to his cage.

Next, Piotr went to Jan's cage, unlocked the door, and motioned with his finger. There was nothing for Jan to do but obey.

Piotr grabbed Jan's shoulder and led him to the place where Petrenko had been sweeping, an open space with two stainless steel tanks and metal debris pushed next to the building wall, along with a half dozen mounds of dirt, products of the priest's work.

Piotr took something from his coat pocket and handed it to Jan: an old toothbrush. The guard tapped on the floor several times with his stick and said loud enough for the others to hear, "Kneel; polish the floor. This is what happens to little dogs that make trouble."

Jan didn't wait for a jab with the stick. He fell to his knees and began brushing the floor, which was begrimed with yellow-gray tallow. Jan's scrubbing with the tiny brush, no matter how assiduous, did nothing to erase the stain.

Within minutes, Jan's bony knees began to hurt. When he tried shifting his weight to relieve some of the pressure from the more painful knee, Piotr grabbed him by the scruff of the neck and leaned in close to his face. "Listen," the guard whispered hurriedly, "tonight you can escape."

Escape? Was this a trick? Jan could not believe what he was hearing.

"You are too slow!" Piotr shouted, painfully close to Jan's ear. The guard gave Jan a shake and shoved him to the ground, and as he pulled him back up, he whispered, "When the others are asleep, look for Petrenko above your cage. Yes, above it!"

Although confused, Jan resumed his painful task with renewed energy. After another thirty minutes, Piotr put his stick under Jan's armpit, signifying that he wanted Jan to stand. After being locked in the same position for so long, Jan struggled to his feet as though he were an old man rising from his prayers. Piotr led him back to the cage, spat on him, and marched out.

"What did he say to you?" Drewniak asked.

"You heard enough of it. Perhaps the major decided that the floor needed polishing. Perhaps Piotr has a toothache and blames it on the brush."

"You are becoming a clown like me, Skala", Drewniak said. "Next, we go mad like Nagy."

As the day progressed, Lutz rallied a little. Petrenko had retained a crust of bread, and Lutz consumed it without any ill effects. Several times, Jan tried to catch Petrenko's eye, but the priest wouldn't cooperate.

Along with the evening meal, Piotr and Evgeny brought the major into the abattoir. At the Lutz-Petrenko cage, the guards filled just one bowl. Then Evgeny pointed his stick at Petrenko, who was standing well away from the door.

"Now", Evgeny said.

Petrenko shuddered as he stepped toward the squat guard who had given him such a severe beating.

"Where are you taking him?" Chan inquired.

"Perhaps you want to come with him, Charlie", replied the major.

Petrenko paused at the cage door and raised his eyes to the roof, saying, "May you see and love in me an iota of what you see and love in your son."

Evgeny prodded him from behind with his stick, and Petrenko followed the Russians out of the building.

A dazed Lutz looked after them uncomprehendingly, but Nagy said loudly, "Good riddance!"

"That should have been you", Schreiber remarked. "The priest might be a fool, but he is not a maggot like you."

"Perhaps he will return", Drewniak said. "Chan returned. Skala returned. And I returned."

Chan seemed more troubled than Jan had ever seen him before. He grasped the fence and climbed all the way to the barbed wire before he stopped his ascent.

"Down, man," Schreiber said, "or they will come for you too."

Like a child, Chan obeyed and sat down against the fence.

The gunshots in the yard were loud enough to hear above the music. None of the men said a word, and all of them except Chan curled up on the floor beneath their blankets. Many of them covered their necks and heads in whatever way they could.

Jan rested on his back, staring up. He didn't care if he was cold, and he didn't care if he was uncomfortable. In fact, the more uncomfortable he was, the less likely he would fall asleep. *Look for Petrenko above your cage!* But Petrenko was dead, so how could the priest help him escape? The answer came to him in a flash as he remembered Petrenko's reference to Dumas' story. Could such a desperate scheme have any hope of being successful?

How many hours later, Jan could not say, but as on the night of the wolf attack, the lights suddenly went out. No one stirred, as far as Jan could tell, not even Chan, who was still sitting upright. Jan stood up and scanned the space above his cage.

Someone was moving on the catwalk directly above him, and the man lowered a body, bound by a rope, into Jan's cage. As Jan dressed the dead Petrenko in his own clothes, he was grateful that someone had already closed the man's eyes and staunched the blood from his recent wounds. Jan then concealed the man's head with his blanket. For the first time since his incarceration, Jan was grateful for the music that covered the noise he could not avoid making. Down came a smaller bundle containing a uniform, boots, hat, and a winter coat and gloves.

Out of the corner of his eye, Jan saw Schreiber roll over, and he peered in the dark at Chan, whose eyes seemed to be open and watching him. Was the Chinese awake? Would he or any of the others call out? Attempting to button the shirt with fumbling fingers, Jan began to fear that this mad plan was another of the major's games, a scheme to demoralize Jan, or perhaps to create a pretense for executing him.

Jan clasped the rope tightly as Piotr pulled him up and onto the catwalk. The guard led Jan to a rear door hidden from the prisoners' view and, once outside, whispered in his native tongue, "This is a sergeant major's uniform. Petrenko said you speak Russian like a

Russian. You had better, or we are both dead men. Stand still while I clip your hair and shave you. I will make a poor job of it, but we must hope for the best ... don't move, I say, or I will cut you. That would finish us. Be bold, for God's sake. The second truck is being sent to Berlin for supplies. Go!"

Although certain that he would be apprehended, Jan felt an odd sense of peace or, perhaps, resignation. If Petrenko and Piotr thought he was worth this sacrifice, he could at least do his part. He shook Piotr's hand, then walked around the corner of the abattoir. Where the snow had been pushed away, the frozen gravel crunched beneath his boots, and Jan felt certain that the sound would betray him.

The cloudy night was moonless and starless. Two trucks, engines running, smoke belching from their tailpipes, were lined up to leave the grounds. As Jan approached the second vehicle, the major and Fyodor stepped from the office into the yard. Jan didn't need to see their faces to recognize them, and he knew that to pause at this moment would give him away. Although expecting to hear a barking challenge, he opened the passenger door of the truck and climbed inside. The driver, wearing the two bars of a junior sergeant, looked at him curiously, and Jan, knowing he outranked the man, said brusquely in his best Russian, "I have a fever. I am seeing the doctor in Berlin."

The driver moved as close to his door as possible and put the truck in gear.

The two trucks crept along the road until the abattoir receded into the darkness behind them. "*Au revoir*, Chateau d'If, Jan Skala", the major had said to him. Dantes had been smuggled *out* of prison as a dead body, whereas Jan owed this tenuous chance for freedom to a dead body being smuggled *in*.

When the trucks came to a fork in the road, they each went their separate ways, and Jan put his head against the cold window and closed his eyes.

They passed through two checkpoints on the road, consisting of no more than lamps on wooden poles and several vehicles. Each time, the driver said a few words to the guard, and they were waved on. After the second of these checks, Jan succumbed to sleep.

Exiting the pavement onto a dirt road awakened Jan. Seeing that it was still dark, he barked at the driver, "Time?"

The man glanced at his wristwatch and said, "Almost eight, sir."

The truck came to a stop at what looked like a makeshift camp rather than a military installation that had been commandeered from the Germans. The road was rutted, frozen dirt rather than paved. The driver exited the truck, leaving Jan alone. Walking to and fro in front of the truck were Russian soldiers and their officers, and Jan was at a loss as to what to do. The gray light of dawn was turning pink, and Jan knew he needed to act quickly before the full light of day placed him in grave peril. Fluent in Russian or not, if he remained with these soldiers for long he would quickly be found out.

What Piotr had told him led Jan to hope that they were in the vicinity of Berlin. There was no other choice but to leave this place and hope that he might be rescued by American or British forces. Bache had said that the Americans were on the southwest side of Berlin. Even freezing to death in the open or being shot in the back while trying to escape was better than being recaptured and returned to the major. Jan opened the truck door and stepped outside. He was groggy, but the cold air and being on his feet again revived him. Lacking a plan, he began walking toward the perimeter of the camp, as if he had a purpose. No one questioned him; those with whom he crossed paths looked sullen and weary.

Jan remembered Piotr's words: "Be bold, for God's sake!" He stopped to pick up a heavy iron crowbar, as if he had work to do, and carried it to the edge of the encampment. A soldier with a flashlight, acting as a sentry, was pacing back and forth between Jan and the woods beyond. Jan waited for the soldier to pass; then he made for the trees.

There was snow in patches, but it wasn't deep. Jan's feet hurt from the too-large boots, but at least his hands and feet were warm. He leaned against a large trunk and looked into the woods. This was no-man's land in every sense of the word, and he was an escaped prisoner in a Russian uniform, minutes from full sunrise and certain capture, not knowing where, or if, succor could be found. He turned around to see the flashlight bobbing in the guard's hand as the man walked away and realized how fortunate he was to have been conveyed to a make-shift camp, rather than a secure military installation. Holding onto the crowbar, Jan set off into the forest in the direction opposite the dawn.

After walking for miles, having crossed a handful of bombed-out roads and tramped through patches of wind-driven snow, at last Jan saw a sign for Berlin. What a relief, for with the sky still overcast, he was sure he had been going in circles. Jan followed the road to Berlin while remaining out of sight behind the trees. He came across an abandoned Nazi panzer with a damaged track. It was no warmer inside the tank, but he discovered uneaten rations under one of the seats: a meat tin he couldn't open with his frozen fingers, in spite of the gloves he had been wearing, and several hard biscuits that he pitched into with avidity. When he finished, he clambered out and slaked his thirst with a handful of snow, knowing this would chill him but desperate for water.

Jan was tempted to return to the tank for a rest, but he knew that if he fell asleep inside of it he would succumb to the cold and never wake up. He must push on, he decided, convinced that a night in the open would be the end of him, and he reduced his thoughts to the single idea of putting one foot in front of the other. Remembering the wolves made him feel more energetic.

On the outskirts of the city, the road was barricaded with a cross-hatched wooden barrier leaning against a truck. A few other trucks flanked the side of the road. Men were milling about, most carrying rifles. Some were smoking cigarettes, something Jan had rarely seen at the abattoir. Looking more closely, he saw a white star on many of the vehicles, and on one "USA" followed by a string of numbers.

Jan realized that his Russian uniform was no longer a lifeline, but a hindrance to the liberty he so desperately sought. Still, how could he let this opportunity pass? Would he ever have a better chance to regain his freedom? And where else could he go with the day waning and night on the way?

Raising his hands high above his head, Jan abandoned the cover of the forest and walked to the road. His heart was pounding, and his mouth was dry. One of the soldiers saw him and shouted something Jan couldn't make out. Two more joined him and walked up the road in Jan's direction, all with rifles trained on him. Though his mind was muddled by dehydration and fatigue, he couldn't ignore the possibility of this becoming a black comedy in which he was shot to death by the very people he had been seeking.

When the soldiers were close enough to hear him, he said in English, "I am not Russian. I am Czech."

"Sure you are, buddy", one answered. "Tired of fighting? Who isn't? We're not the Red Cross. Come on, and keep those hands up high."

As Jan walked into the heart of the checkpoint, he saw that there were more trucks and other military vehicles than he had been able to see from the forest, most in a depression, a vale, below the road. Within this lower area, large tents had been assembled, and several tanks were stationed on the perimeter of the camp. The soldiers led Jan inside a tent, where an officer sitting behind a desk looked up at him and raised his eyebrows.

"Says he's Czech, not Russian, sir", said the soldier. "He speaks English."

"Where did you find him, Corporal?" asked the officer.

"He found us, sir. Came out of the woods."

"I can't let you into the American zone", the lieutenant said to Jan. "No Russian deserters. You're not the first Russian soldier who's come knocking at our door. We must return you to your people."

"I tell you, I am not Russian. I am Czech."

"Can you prove you are Czech?"

Jan wanted to explain that he had no identification because he had been in a Russian prison, but thought better of it and shook his head.

"My orders say no one passes without proper papers, and certainly no one wearing a Russian uniform."

"If you send me back to the Russians, they will kill me."

"You should have considered that when you ran away", the lieutenant said suspiciously. Then the young man sat back, looked hard at

Jan for several seconds, and said, "You look like you've had a tough time of it. Would you like a cup of coffee?"

Noticing the pot on the desk, Jan said, "I would be grateful."

Jan could not believe how good this tepid, sediment-laden coffee tasted. He had removed his gloves, and now he encircled the metal cup with both hands.

"What's going on here?" asked another voice, belonging to a big-boned, red-faced officer.

"This man says he's Czech, sir. He has no papers, and as you can see, he's wearing a Russian uniform."

"What brings you to Berlin?" the officer asked Jan.

Jan couldn't say why he felt compelled to tell this man the truth. "I am a Czech citizen, a journalist. The Russians arrested me and held me at a site east of Berlin because they believed I had information about Soviet prison camps."

"Where did you get the Russian uniform?"

"From a Russian guard at the place where I was being held."

"Hmmm," said the man eyeing Jan up and down, "everyone I talk to these days is innocent, or so they say. Still, your English is better than a Russian sergeant's ought to be; curious that. Lieutenant, write this man a pass." Addressing Jan, he asked, "What's your name?"

"Jan Skala."

"Come with me, Skala. I want you to meet some friends of mine."

June 20, 1990

"I have come to kill you. I have come to kill both of you."

"Kill us? Who are you?" Jan demanded. A sharp pain seized his chest. A defective heart, the doctors had told him; nothing to be done except to take one of the nitroglycerin pills in his pocket. Was this ailment also a residue of his imprisonment, as were his damaged feet, which always throbbed when the weather turned cold?

"I am Drewniak, and if I am not mistaken, you are Skala and Piotr."

"Drewniak?" Jan said in a hushed tone, searching the old man's features for something recognizable. "Why do you want to kill us?"

"He knows why", answered Drewniak, nodding at Piotr.

Piotr looked down at his glass, and the rain began to pound against the fabric of the umbrella like a man beating a drum.

"If this Russian will not speak, then I will tell you, Skala. The major needed a scapegoat, and the explanation that I slept through your escape from a locked cage, and that I had no knowledge of how it was done, was impossible to defend.

"Our dear major put me in a Russian labor camp for fifteen years, and that place was worse than the abattoir. When I was finally released, I could find no trace of Danuta. You remember, Skala, my dear wife. Maybe she is in America or Canada, and maybe she is in the ground. You, both of you, are responsible for this."

Jan's heart was still thumping; his chest was constricting. "But ... Drewniak—"

"I had ample time to think while I was in prison", Drewniak continued. "You," said the Pole, glaring at Piotr, "you must have communicated the scheme to Skala while he was cleaning the floor with the brush."

The rain was pelting the cement, and water was pooling around the men's shoes. All of the other customers had either left the café or gone inside. The proprietor was watching them from the doorway, but he made no move to approach their table.

"An acquaintance in Dublin learned that you intended to travel to Berlin", Drewniak said to Jan. "I have known your whereabouts for many years, but my ability to travel has been . . . restricted. Doors are now opening, and many unfortunates who could not escape are finally free.

"I did not know what you planned to do here in Berlin, but I hoped a meeting with the person who helped you escape might have been arranged. I had my suspicions about who this person might be, but I could not be certain. Even if you were not meeting this person, I told myself, I could still settle accounts with you."

"I will get you something to drink", Piotr said to Drewniak, rising out of his chair.

Drewniak's eyes blazed. "You will go nowhere! Buildings have backdoors. What I have come to do requires a clear head. I am an old man—a broken man—but I will do what I set out to do, God help me."

"We never intended for anyone else to suffer", Jan said.

"I remember how you used to say foolish things", Drewniak countered. "You knew the major, and you knew that someone would pay for your escape. Everything went better than you could have hoped. When the morning meal was served, you were thought to be ill, and no one disturbed the blanket that covered Petrenko's chest and head until later. Since he was wearing your clothes and you were nearly the same size, there was no reason to be suspicious."

Drewniak removed his hat, revealing a full head of white hair, shook the hat violently, and replaced it on his head, before saying to Piotr, "Did you not realize the risk you were taking? A hundred things might have gone wrong. If you had been found out, you would have met with a terrible death. You know how angry the major became—like a madman—when he learned about the escape."

"It was a risk I was willing to take", Piotr replied.

Drewniak muttered something Jan couldn't hear before saying, "I understand Skala taking the risk, but why would you agree to such madness?"

Piotr grinned at the Pole and said, "Because Father Petrenko had asked me to do it, not because I had any hope that we would succeed. I thought that I would be found out and executed."

"How long had you been working with the priest?" an amazed Drewniak asked Piotr.

"Why, from the beginning, when he arrived at the abattoir. He needed a few drops of wine for Mass, which I provided in waxed-over thimbles. The idea for Skala's escape was his, but he needed my assistance. Afterward, there were anxious days, but it was common knowledge that I was too stupid and simple to have accomplished such a marvel."

"He trusted you?" Drewniak asked the Russian.

"We trusted each other, he and I", the old Russian said rhapsodically.

Drewniak laughed bitterly. "We all thought that Petrenko was a fool, and he made fools out of us. He made a fool out of me."

"Not everything went as desired. Chan saw everything", Jan announced, surprising both men.

"The prisoners were questioned", Piotr said. "Chan could not have revealed what he saw, or I would have been arrested. So you see, Drewniak, someone saw the escape; not everything went as planned. Fortunately, it was Chan, an *honorable* man.

"As it was, I was interviewed by the major himself, the worst hour of my life. I told lie after lie, every minute expecting to be accused and dragged away. This was my finest moment as ... ah ... dimwit. Yes, as a dimwit, boring the major with prattle and stupid questions."

Jan listened in amazement. For decades, he had known that Piotr was bold and courageous, but this performance, given the major Jan remembered, must have been a tour de force. After what Piotr had risked to obtain Jan's freedom, Jan could not restrain himself from responding to Drewniak's imprecations. "There is a reason that it was you who paid for my escape," Jan said to Drewniak, "and not just because we shared the same cage. If Katrina was a Russian informer, I asked myself, why not another? In my meetings with the major, he warned me to be wary of you, a ploy to make me believe that he distrusted you. Perhaps the reason you were dealt with so harshly by the major was not his suspicion that you had helped me to escape, but that you had failed to learn from me what he wanted to know."

To Jan, Drewniak now looked less the hunter and more the hunted. The Pole's eyes were restless, and more than once his lips moved as if he were speaking to himself. Drewniak, glancing at Piotr, said, "The risks were ... ah ... outrageous, but your good fortune, and my bad fortune, held out."

Bad fortune? During all those years, when the Soviet empire was strong, Jan had never left the British Isles for fear that his enemies might still be searching for him. Jan had known that if he had been more courageous he might have found a way back to Fran, or found a way to bring her to him. In recent years, he had told himself that his fear was irrational, but this reticence to leave his safe haven had remained. Now, with the Soviet empire dissolving, he had ventured out, and bad fortune had caught up with *him*.

The rain had subsided, but the backs of the three men, in spite of the table umbrella and Drewniak's hat, were dark with water. Jan could not believe that this dilapidated old man had cared enough to seek them out after all these years.

"It is a miracle you were not caught and executed", Drewniak said to Piotr.

"I have often thought so", the Russian replied.

"What made Skala worth the risk?"

Piotr looked Jan in the eye and said, "He was my opportunity to redeem *myself*. I told myself that during my time in the army I was only following orders, only doing what I was forced to do. Yet I have many terrible memories of the war and that prison, many regrets; but always I try to remember this good thing I have done."

"Hah! That priest bewitched you!" Drewniak said, pounding his fist on the table. "Yet Skala escaped, you were never found out, and

I was sent to that Russian camp. Perhaps that man put a curse on me. Well, no matter; I am here to get justice."

"Killing us is not justice … but murder," said Jan, "as were the killings of Brio, Petrenko, and the others."

"I did not kill them," Drewniak protested, shaking his head, "and they were not murdered. Those men—every one of them—were enemies of socialism."

"Brio said we were brought together for a reason", Jan observed.

Drewniak smiled at him slyly and said, "Brio was a poet, a dreamer."

"Weren't we all commanded to speak English because this was the only foreign language you and Katrina understood?"

"Enough of this! You are desperate to save yourself. I am your enemy!"

"*You* have made that choice", Jan retorted, still feeling a shortness of breath. Long ago he had admitted, first to himself and then to others, that his behavior in the war, his own choices, had been vile, cowardly, reprehensible. There was a time when he couldn't stand himself, when his skin crawled whenever he looked in a mirror. Because he couldn't relive the past, he had decided to do the next best thing, perhaps an even better thing: forgive.

Drewniak opened his mouth as if to say something, closed it again, and adjusted his hat. At that moment, a section of the Wall crashed into the pavement. Startled, Jan pushed back the chair and stood up. Feeling a stabbing pain, he clutched his chest and groaned.

"What is wrong?" Piotr asked him.

Jan reached inside his coat, fumbling to locate his shirt pocket.

"Here, let me help!" a woman on the street called out in German, dropping her umbrella on the pavement and hurrying to their table.

"The pill in my pocket", Jan whispered, trying to calm himself.

She pulled his hand away from the coat, unbuttoned it, and found the pill in his shirt pocket. "Open your mouth", she said, coaxing him back into his chair.

Gradually, the pressure in Jan's chest lessened. He could breathe again, though with effort. She kept her finger on his wrist, measuring his pulse, while he recovered from the spell.

Looking at the woman for the first time, Jan was reminded of Fran, not because she was a lookalike but in the way she carried herself, her decisiveness, and in her probing eyes.

The woman said in German, "You should be seen by a doctor."

"English, please", Drewniak said curtly.

She hesitated before saying in English, "Can I call someone, an ambulance?"

Jan said to her, "It is kind of you to ask, but no, thank you. The doctors can do no more than supply me with these pills."

The proprietor and several others had come outside to see what the disturbance was about. Jan observed that Drewniak, whose lips were now quivering, had dropped his linen over the pistol.

"Do you live in Berlin?" Jan asked the woman.

She nodded, looking toward the Wall. "These are carnival days for us. And you?"

"Visitors", Jan answered, convinced that she was engaging him in conversation as a pretext for making sure he had recovered. "We were here together in 1945."

She gave him a curious stare and said, "Those were terrible days to be in Germany."

"We were fortunate to survive."

"Some more fortunate than others", Drewniak said bitterly. Seeing water dripping from Jan's chin, the woman retrieved her umbrella and extended it so that he was protected from the rain. She was watching Jan closely as she said, "I was born in West Berlin, but we had relatives in the DDR we were once able to visit. I remember a big government building in Dresden where they made us wait for hours. I was near ten; it was 1969, about. Soldiers walked from one end of the building to the other, back and forth with their rifles. I was so frustrated that I marched to the bust of Lenin in the center of the building and stuck out my tongue." She laughed lightheartedly. "In the blink of an eye, my mother and grandmother rushed over and gathered me up."

Piotr began chuckling and patted her on the hand.

"Were you soldiers?" she asked them.

"I am a Polish patriot!" Drewniak said defiantly. Was the claim true, or had the Pole lived with the story so long that it had acquired the semblance of truth?

Jan said to the woman, "Thank you for your kindness, but you have spent enough time with old men who do not know enough to get out of the rain. I am better now."

The woman didn't look convinced. "Promise me you will get out of the rain and into bed for a rest."

"Yes, I promise. We are finishing our ... business."

After the woman reluctantly left them, the men sat facing each other, like three granite statues, waiting for someone to act, to do something. It was impossible for Jan to guess what Drewniak was thinking, but whatever confidence the Pole had brought with him to the table had evaporated. The napkin over the hand with the gun trembled, and his eyes kept darting to the proprietor, who was watching them from the doorway.

"If you are going to kill us," Piotr said to Drewniak, "you had best get it over with."

"Yes, Jerzy," Jan said, his lightheadedness making him feel bold, "this pill might not keep me alive for long."

Drewniak turned his head toward the Wall, and in his profile Jan could see something of the man who had shared his cage in the abattoir.

Without looking at either of the men or saying another word, the Pole rose stiffly from his chair. Like an old vagabond he shuffled down the street in the rain.

Jan and Piotr watched Drewniak until he turned a corner.

"Time to go", Piotr said, taking a hold of Jan's arm. "I will see you to your hotel."

The Russian helped Jan to his feet, and Jan placed a wad of Deutschmarks on the table. Both men left the pistol on the chair where the old man had abandoned it.